C000045411

MURDER

Recent Titles by Jeffrey Ashford from Severn House

THE COST OF INNOCENCE
AN HONEST BETRAYAL
MURDER WILL OUT
A WEB OF CIRCUMSTANCES

MURDER WILL OUT

Jeffrey Ashford

This first world edition published in Great Britain 2000 by
SEVERN HOUSE PUBLISHERS LTD of
9–15 High Street, Sutton, Surrey SM1 1DF.
This first world edition published in the USA 2000 by
SEVERN HOUSE PUBLISHERS INC of
595 Madison Avenue, New York, N.Y. 10022.

British Library Cataloguing in Publication Data

Ashford, Jeffrey, 1926–
    Murder will out
    1. Hit-and-run drivers - Great Britain - Fiction
    2. Detective and mystery stories
    I.   Title
    823.9'14 [F]

    ISBN 0-7278-5563-8

Typeset by Hewer Text Ltd.,
Edinburgh, Scotland.
Printed and bound in Great Britain by
MPG Books Ltd, Bodmin, Cornwall.

One

"What's got you looking like you died yesterday?" Parr asked loudly, as if his listener were in the next room rather than a few feet away.

"I woke up this morning, looked in the mirror and found I had," Keen replied.

"Had what?"

He didn't bother to reply. If conversation with Parr was not about rugger or women, it tended to become laboured.

"Cheer up, mate, you can only die once."

"It's the getting there that worries me."

Cain stepped through the open doorway of the CID general room. "The Guv'nor's shouting for the GCB. Where is it and why wasn't it on his desk?"

The first DC to arrive in the morning was supposed, after relieving the night duty DC, to collect up the Grid Crime Book and put it on the detective inspector's desk so he could inspect it and assign which DC was to investigate what case. Parr had been the first to arrive, but in matters of routine his memory was poor.

"Struck dumb, are we?"

"If we weren't real dumb, Sarge, we wouldn't be doing this job," Parr said.

Cain was not amused. "Get it to him bloody smart." He turned on his heels and left.

Parr stood and searched the tops of the several desks until he found the thick book in ugly brown covers. "There's a man

1

who'd win a triple rollover lottery and still count his change from a quid." He left, taking with him an air of good-natured turmoil.

Maybe Cain was someone else who had precious little in life to smile about, Keen thought. He wondered if Parr had ever considered the possibility that not everyone passed through life blind to its darker moments. It would have been nice to have possessed a little of that blindness when Anne had left home earlier . . .

He switched on the computer and printer on his desk, opened one of the folders, began to type. Inevitably, he hit the wrong keys from time to time and occasionally the screen darkened, margins altered, wanted spaces disappeared, unwanted ones appeared . . . He was a good detective, but a poor computer operator.

He finished the work, corrected mistakes (causing more mistakes which had to be corrected which caused more mistakes . . .) and set the printer to work. As it chattered away, his mind drifted. Yesterday had been tough going and at the end of it he had joined Barrat and Soper at one of their usual locals to drink away some of the stress. About to leave, a couple of PCs in civvies had joined them and time had slid. When he'd arrived home, Anne had been wearing her arctic expression. Even after several years of marriage, it still astonished him that she could summon up such cold anger. Where had he been all evening? He'd explained that a late job had come in and held him back. "Really?" she'd said. "Then whoever spoke to me on the phone and said you'd gone off duty a couple of hours before was wrong?" He'd silently cursed her informant for breaking one of the basic rules of good policing – never give a wife the chance to bitch. He admitted he'd spent a little time in a pub. "Drinking yourself stupid being so much more important than remembering you'd promised Judy you'd be home in time to read her new book to her before she went to sleep?" He'd started to explain that he'd had one hell of a day

2

and had been so stressed out . . . "Your family doesn't mean a thing to you. Judy and I take a back seat when it comes to boozing." He'd said she didn't understand. "Too right, I don't. And you don't understand what it is I don't understand." This had foxed him and, ill advised, he'd said so. "Because you've drunk so much you can't think straight." From the specific, she'd moved on to the general. He preferred to be with his mates rather than his own family because his loyalty was to them. Provoked by what he'd drunk, his shamed defence had become anger. How could she talk such nonsense? "Because you prove it day after day, or should I say, night after night? How many times in the last week have you come straight back here after finishing work? Just tell me that." He'd suggested every night but the past one. He was a liar and like all the others, saw her as a cook and bed-warmer, nothing more. So she'd finally had enough and was going to leave him. Comforting himself with the thought that in the morning she'd be more reasonable, he'd said good night (ignored) as she swept into the spare bedroom.

When she'd put eggs and bacon on fried bread in front of him this morning, she'd said that she and Judy were going to stay with Fay until she could decide exactly what her future would be. Annoyed, in part because he was trying to keep a sense of guilt at bay, he'd made the mistake of telling her not to get worked up over nothing. He should have remembered some of the best advice a man could receive – never look a spitting cobra in the eye or tell a woman she was being irrational. In an even more glacial tone, she'd told him she would be driving Judy to school and returning to collect her things. And he could turn off the gas under the coffee because she'd finished being his domestic slave. As she'd swept out of the room, he'd wondered why she'd cooked his breakfast.

"I'm sorry to disturb you," Cain said, with heavy sarcasm, from the doorway, "but if you could be kind enough to find the time to do something for me, I'd be grateful."

3

"Sure, Sarge."

"There's a report just in of a hit-and-run at Two Oaks crossroads, north of Kingsholte. No further details. And this time, don't forget to enter up the duty book before you take off." He left, the heavy features of his round, puffy face registering congenital discontent.

Keen consigned the completed work to "Save", hoping he had not done anything, or failed to do something, which would ensure a blank screen in the future. He searched for the Duty Book, found it under a pile of divisional crime information sheets. In it, he wrote down the time, destination, and reason for his call-out. He took the lift down to the ground floor, left the building through the rear entrance. There were no waiting CID cars, so he crossed to his Astra, settled behind the wheel and on the left-hand page of the diary noted down the milometer reading – car expenses would be recorded on the right-hand side. He started the engine, reversed, drove up to the exit to find the flow of passing traffic was heavy.

Women, he decided, had never understood male bonding because they enjoyed no equivalent – the knowledge that one would be backed up as quickly and readily as one would back up, the comradeship that willingly shared both pleasures and dangers, the satisfaction of being part of a small, self-contained elite. Us and them. Them, the politicians, the lawyers, the bleeding-heart liberals . . .

The road cleared and he drew out. Down to the T-junction, turn right to pass the railway station, across the small river, and along a road bordered by a relatively new housing estate in which a policeman in uniform on his own could well be in danger.

As he reached the countryside, the clouds thinned to allow sunshine to reach down and brighten the fields, hedges, copses . . . His father had been a tenant farmer who had had to struggle to make any sort of a living because he had not had enough land and that which he had was largely heavy clay that

4

in wet weather possessed the consistency of glue and in dry
weather, concrete. His father had discouraged him from farm-
ing on the grounds that since politicians' principles followed
the votes, and the majority of the population lived in towns,
the welfare of the countryside and those who lived in it would
always be of small moment. He'd joined the police. Looking
back was to be sardonically amused; he'd actually believed
that by enforcing law and order, he would earn the public's
gratitude. Sixty or more years out of date. For the public, all
authority had become "Them".

As he drew level with the northern boundary of a wood, a
young cock pheasant, beginning to colour, nearly committed
suicide as it flew out in front of his car, voiding as it went.
When younger, he'd enjoyed shooting on his father's land
(contrary to the terms of the lease), but Anne was from the
town and hated the thought of killing in the name of sport,
and before their marriage he'd put his old hammer Holland &
Holland to rest. Len Parr defined marriage as unconditional
surrender . . .

There were four oaks at Two Oaks crossroads – the name
dated back more than four hundred years and the present trees
were less than two hundred years old. A police "Slow" notice
had been set out some way before cones reduced the width of
the road by half. A civilian with two cameras slung around his
neck stood near the verge, a man in a white boiler suit was
using a rake to search the grass and weeds on the verge, a PC
near a police car was talking to an elderly woman, and a
handful of onlookers were grouped on the opposite side of the
road.

He parked beyond the police car. The PC briefly greeted
him, resumed speaking to the woman. He gazed at the nearest
field, at the far end of which grew two of the four oaks. His
father had died several years before, but he had only to be in
the countryside to recall him. His father had been a man of
slow speech and set mind, who had enjoyed an unusual affinity

with animals; once, he had walked up to a cow panicked to the point of becoming dangerous and had calmed it merely by speech and touch . . .

The woman walked away. The PC crossed to where Keen stood. "Not seen you for a time, Mike. So how's the world treating you?"

"With a kick in the crutch."

"Don't you lads in CID ever smile?"

"It's being miserable that keeps us happy . . . What's the score here?"

"The victim's name is Noyes, lives in a house just around the corner." The PC pointed at the curve in the road beyond where they stood. "Seems he was walking down to the crossroads, got hit by a car and thrown up on to the grass verge; there's the marker." He indicated a small white stake. "According to the paramedic, he's pretty well smashed up and will be lucky to live."

"He was walking towards the crossroads?"

"That's right."

"How do we know that?"

"Miss Logan – as she pointed out very sharply when I called her Mrs Logan – was in her garden when he went past. She's the old biddy I was talking to a moment ago."

"So he was hit from behind?"

"From the front."

"That doesn't make sense, since he'd have been on the right-hand side of the road to an oncoming car."

"Sense or not, that's the picture."

Keen stared at the marker. For a car to have hit Noyes head on, it would have had to be right over on the wrong side of the road. A drunken driver? It seemed too early in the morning. Speed? If the driver had come straight across the crossroads, he would have had the victim in sight for maybe six hundred yards and only if he'd lost control would he have come right across the road – if that had happened, surely he'd have

6

braked so fiercely that there would have been tyre marks on the road? There were none. Had he turned into this road so quickly that the car had dry skidded? "Have you checked for marks back at the crossroads?"

"Yeah. There aren't any."

Experience suggested it was probably a mistake to assume that because the facts seemed to contradict each other, one or more of them had to be incorrect; it could well be the conclusion that was wrong. "Did Miss Logan see the collision?"

"She was pruning a rose when Noyes walked past. She went up the side of her bungalow and heard a heavy thump and a cry. She returned to see what had happened and saw Noyes lying on the verge with his feet just on the road. The car was up to the bend."

"On the left-hand side of the road."

"Can't say I asked."

"Can she identify the make of car or did she get any part of the number?"

"It was light grey and that's as far as I could get her to go. She rang nine nine nine, then went over to where Noyes lay, but as she said, there wasn't anything she could do for him."

"Do we know anything about Noyes? Is he married?"

"His wife died a few years back and there aren't any children."

"So he lives on his own?"

"From time to time. According to the old girl, who sounds like she disapproves of a bloke enjoying life, he often entertains the ladies. Only she made it clear they weren't ladies."

"Is anyone staying with him now?"

"She doesn't know."

"What about relatives?"

"She only knows of a niece, who she met once. The name's Laura, but that's all she can tell us about her."

"Had she anything more to say about him?"

"Only some waffle about his often going off on cruises and then insisting on telling her all about them."

"If there isn't anyone in the house right now, I'm going to have to force an entry to see if I can trace this Laura, so let's move."

"You don't need me."

"I have to have a witness for a break-in."

The PC bad-temperedly accepted that he would have to accompany Keen.

When they were halfway around the bend, Noyes's house came in sight. Subconsciously, and irrationally, Keen had expected a small, cramped house or bungalow, built to a tight budget; what he saw was a two-hundred-year-old farmhouse, part brick, part clapboard, with a steeply pitched peg-tile roof and a large central chimney. "A nice place," he said.

"Nice for what? Live out here and what's there to do?"

He didn't try to answer. Town was town and country was country and never the twain could meet.

They approached the front garden and Keen was surprised and vaguely irritated to see it was a miniature jungle of weeds and overgrown grass. To have the privilege of living in such a house carried the responsibility of maintaining a well-kept garden – or so he thought, aware there were those who would call such a sentiment romantic nonsense.

He knocked on the front door, rang the bell. There was no response. He tried the handle; unsurprisingly, the door was locked. He led the way round to the back. Where – in his view – there should have been a kitchen garden was a field surrounded by a thorn hedge which had not been trimmed the previous winter. He knocked on the "stable" back door. If someone had been seriously injured and it proved impossible to ascertain the name of a relative any other way, an officer had the right to break into the house. (Naturally, an endless succession of forms had later to be filled in to justify such action.) He picked up a small rock that marked the edge of the weed-infested gravel path, used that to smash the window to the right of the door. Having cleared all slivers of glass, he reached inside and, at full stretch, was able to unbolt the top half of the door. Since the bottom half was locked and there was no key inside – Noyes must have left this way and pocketed the key – he climbed over it.

Traditionally, the kitchen of a man living on his own was a graveyard of unwashed dishes, pots, pans, plates, cups, saucers, and cutlery, and the state of the garden could have been thought to reinforce that tradition; the kitchen was almost in show-room condition.

Large refrigerator/deep freeze, washing and washing-up machines, microwave oven, electric stove with ceramic top, juicer, food mixer . . . Anne had been wanting a new food mixer for some time because the present one was— Keen jerked his mind away from such thoughts. "OK, we'll start in the hall and then go upstairs."

The telephone stood on a small table; in the single deep drawer were the two volumes of the local directory, but no personal record of frequently used numbers.

They climbed the steep stairs. There were three bedrooms. One contained little but dust; the second had a bed, a chest-of-drawers on which stood a cracked vanity mirror, and an air which suggested it was seldom occupied; the third occasioned their astonishment. The king-sized bed had above it, fixed to the ceiling, a large circular mirror.

"I've heard of this sort of thing, but never before met it," observed the PC. "A man who likes to see what he's doing as well as who!" He sat on the bed and looked up. "It's not all that clear."

"Perhaps he uses binoculars."

He stood, went around the bed, and studied the very large television set on its stand. "I saw one like this in that upmarket store in the High Street. It's digital, analogue, alters the shape of the picture, and probably dances a jig if you ask it to. As I remember it, there's no change from fifteen hundred quid. Noyes isn't short of the odd penny." Next to the television was a glass-fronted cabinet containing a number of videotapes. He brought one out, whistled as he stared at the cover. "What a naughty girl! Have a look at this and see what it does to your blood pressure." He lobbed the tape over.

On the front, several photographs, in a montage, were unambiguous; more photographs on the back were even more explicit.

"If they're all the same," the PC said, "he'll likely not have the energy to watch the news." He examined a second tape. "Different technique, same conclusion . . . At twenty-five quid, or more, each one, he's spent a small fortune on his hobby."

Keen dropped the first tape onto the bed. "How about getting back to work?"

"Spoilsport!"

There were still people who hid things under the mattress. Keen lifted it up, to be initially caught out by its weight. There was nothing under it. He moved to the left-hand bedside table and slid open the shallow drawer. There were several brochures and each one, issued by the same company, covered luxury cruises. Out of curiosity, he checked the cost of a fortnight's fly-and-cruise to Penang, Ko Khai Nok, Koh Similan, and Phuket. A circle in pencil had been drawn around the quotation for the owner's suite. It seemed Noyes did things in style.

He went round the foot of the bed to check the contents of the drawer of the other bedside table. Several packets of condoms, two catalogues from Amsterdam listing pornographic tapes, and, in the sharpest possible contrast, a Christmas card featuring half a dozen children singing carols outside an opened doorway in which stood a couple, a baby in the arms of the wife . . . There was a shout of alarm from the cupboard, the sounds of falling, and then some inspired swearing.

Keen dropped the card on the bed, crossed to the cupboard and looked inside. The PC lay on his side as he tried to kick free a panel of plasterboard. "Bloody thing's wrapped itself around me," he complained, as if it had developed tentacles and a will. "Must have been broken before." That was said defensively. The damage would have to be officially explained.

It was obvious he had inadvertently exposed an irregularly shaped hiding space between the back wall of the cupboard and the brickwork of the central chimney, normally well concealed by the plasterboard. From where he stood, Keen could see the corner of a metal box. "There's something inside – let's have it out."

"You don't want to know if I've broken my ankle?"

"Pass the box out and then tell me."

The PC scrambled into a kneeling position, wrenched the panel off his foot, slid out of the space an old-fashioned deed box. Keen carried this onto the bed. It was not locked. Inside, neatly packed in rows, were several bundles of banknotes, mostly of twenty pounds' denomination. When he lifted out one bundle, it was to find another underneath.

The PC left the cupboard and stood by his side. "You never know your luck!"

"Shades of the Cullinan diamond."

"How's that?"

"As I remember the story, a bloke found it by chance."

"So he retired and lived happily ever after."

"I doubt that. Usually, one person sows, another reaps the profit."

"What are we looking at? Twenty thousand?"

"There's more underneath so we're about to count it all and find out."

"Why us?"

"We have to take it back to the station for safe keeping and you want to know why it's got to be counted?"

"What I'm saying is, why now? I don't need to spend any

more time here. Bert's waiting in the car and he'll go spare if I hang around much longer . . ."

"He'll be fast asleep." Keen picked up the box and, holding back the lid, upended it. There was a cascade of bundles of banknotes plus a booklet with grey covers and a signet ring with a large red stone in an elaborate setting.

The PC picked up the ring. "D'you reckon this is a real ruby?"

"How would I know?"

"If it is, it's likely worth more than I am."

"It doesn't have to be genuine for that."

"Bloody humorous."

Keen put the booklet and ring on the nearer bedside table. He divided the bundles into rough halves, pushed one across. "Let's get started."

Their first counts differed by eighty pounds. The PC suggested they signed for the two totals, called Keen a miserable bastard when he insisted on a second count. This time, their totals agreed. "We'd better have a third go to make certain," Keen said.

"I never thought I'd get fed up counting money, but I'm telling you, I'm calling it a day right now."

Keen accepted this. "I'll make a note of both totals."

"If you're going to do that now, why the hell couldn't you have saved time and done it before?"

He opened his notebook and on the first blank page, noted the facts. He passed the notebook and pen across.

The PC signed his name, straightened up and watched Keen pack away the money. "I wonder if the poor sod will live to buy himself more videos to watch with his girlfriends? . . . I'm on my way." He left.

Keen dropped the ring on top of the money, picked up the booklet. *A Report of the Official Inquiry into the Collision between SS* Slecome Bay *and MV* Atoka. Not exactly the expected reading of a man of Noyes's obvious interests. He put the booklet in the deed box, shut the lid. He was amused by the slight tension he experienced because he was now the guardian, even if only temporarily, of one hundred and sixty-two thousand, seven hundred and fifty pounds in cash.

He carried the box downstairs to the hall and put it on the floor by the side of the table on which was the phone, was about to ring divisional HQ when he remembered he'd forgotten to look inside the Xmas card. He carried the box upstairs. If he'd had handcuffs on him, he would have handcuffed it to his wrist.

He opened the card. The banal, printed greeting was signed Laura. Below was written: "My new address is 24 Sibton Avenue, Richly Cross." Eureka! he silently shouted. She surely had to be the niece Miss Logan had mentioned.

He carried the box downstairs to the hall, dialled divisional HQ, asked to speak to the detective sergeant.

"The victim's been taken to hospital, Sarge. According to the paramedic, he's not looking good; it could easily become causing death by dangerous driving."

"Any line on the car involved?"

"There was only one eyewitness and she didn't see it until it was well away. According to Jay, who questioned her, the best she can do so far is it was light grey."

"Haven't you questioned her to see if she can come up with something more useful?"

"No, because . . ."

"Because it hasn't occurred to you that that might be a good idea."

"Hang on. It didn't seem we'd find out anything without forcing an entry into his place and looking around, so we broke in . . ."

"Then make certain you file a full report. Is there much damage?"

"A broken window and a bust panel of hardboard."

"Have you arranged for repairs to be carried out?"

13

"No, because . . ."

"Because you need bloody spoon-feeding."

"Because we found a hiding place in which was a deed box and in that is a whole heap of banknotes which add up to a hundred and sixty-two thousand . . ."

"A hundred and sixty-two thousand pounds?" Cain's tone expressed his surprise.

"And seven hundred and fifty."

"So where's the money now?"

"At my feet."

"Then keep both of 'em hard on it. Who was with you?"

"Jay. He was in the cupboard in the main bedroom."

"You both counted?"

"Twice. The first time we differed by eighty pounds, the second we agreed."

"Get the money here as quickly as you can move."

"I leave the house unsecured and with a broken window?"

"With that weight of money loose, you don't worry if every window's wide open and there's a notice welcoming Chummy. And when you get here, we'll recount the money with the DI so there's no room for tongues to start wagging."

When the call was over, Keen picked up the deed box. Cain might be morose, quick to blame and slow to praise, but he had an old-fashioned, fierce pride in the force.

Two

C ain was not in his room. Keen put the strong box on the desk, moved a chair away from the wall and sat. He checked the time. 12.15. Anne would have collected Judy from the school and presumably was now driving to Malcolm House where Fay lived with a husband who endlessly spoiled her to try to make up for her barrenness. Fay appeared to flirt with him and openly enjoyed a conversation filled with risqué possibilities. He had sometimes wondered what would happen if he made a serious pass at her; would she respond, as her manner so often suggested, or was it all amusing froth? He'd once put the question, of course with the preamble that he'd no intention of ever finding out, to Anne. Her amusement had been coloured with scorn. When he looked in a mirror, did he see Adonis?

He searched for something to read, but on the desk there were only files, and in the bookcase a few textbooks. He remembered the booklet in the deed box. The report on a collision at sea hardly suggested entertaining reading, but it might at least keep Anne out of his mind for a while. And come to that, why had the booklet been kept in the deed box along with the money and the signet ring?

He opened the box, brought out the report. It was issued to guide shipmasters in the use of radar at sea. The hearing, inquiring into the circumstances attending the collision between SS *Slecome Bay* and MV *Atoka* on the third of October 1963, had been held in London before Mr Torrens

15

Gilmore, QC, sitting as Wreck Commissioner, assisted by Captain Q. Turpin and Captain A. Knight, sitting as assessors. Mr T. Hickman and Mr G. Timms for the Minister of Transport. Mr J. Rowe, QC and Mr Ingham for Captain G. Jordan, master of the *Slecome Bay*. Mr P. Stobe, QC and Mr Halcombe for the Aylton Shipping Company . . .

He turned the pages to the first day's hearing.

THE COMMISSIONER. Yes, Mr Hickman.

MR HICKMAN. The Order for this Formal Investigation, sir. (Order handed in.) On the third of October of last year, the British steamship *Slecome Bay*, of London, Official Number 3468817, was in collision with the British Motor Vessel *Atoka* of Liverpool, Official Number 4176468. Sadly, a shipping casualty was incurred and a preliminary hearing has been held concerning the same. Now, the Minister of Transport in pursuance of the powers invested in him hereby directs that a Formal Investigation be held in the said shipping casualty by a Wreck Commissioner . . .

The *Slecome Bay*, of 12,090 tons gross, sailed at 1352 on the second of October with a crew of fifty-three. She is a twin-screw vessel with two by three reduction geared turbines and two water tube boilers. Her cruising speed is sixteen knots.

Soon after 2000 hours on the 2nd of October visibility deteriorated and the master was called to the bridge. He ordered stand-by to be rung and in accordance with the pre-arranged agreement with the engine room, speed was reduced to approximately twelve knots. The radar was in operation, fog signals were commenced, and a look-out was posted on the fo'c'sle head. The Decca Navigator was thereafter employed to check the ship's position.

At about 0243 hours the following morning, a fresh echo was detected on the PPI at nine miles, bearing ten degrees on the port bow. An almost continuous watch on the approaching vessel was maintained on the radar. The fog signals of the other vessel became audible and then suddenly these became very much louder; fearing a collision, the master ordered the helm hard a port . . .

Laid down in 1939, completed in 1941, torpedoed in 1943 in the South Atlantic but saved by the efforts of master and crew, who patched her damaged hull with wood and concrete and sailed her to the UK where she discharged her cargo of lamb, cheese, and butter, the *Slecome Bay* was from an earlier era and possessed a stubby grace which container ships, with their monstrous deck cargoes, could never enjoy.

Originally one of a fleet of cargo liners, she had been put up for sale at little more than break-up value. She had been bought by Robert Ambrose, branded a fool by his contemporaries for thinking there could be profit in old ships even when bought at bargain prices. Ambrose and Onassis had had one thing in common – the ability to think around and beyond others' judgements. With all her refrigerating equipment removed and hull insulation ripped out, and an itinerary that was sometimes not fixed, she was almost, but not quite, a tramp. She could carry twenty passengers, in comfortable cabins aft of the officers' accommodation; there were some who took passage on her who didn't ask where her destinations probably lay because they still sought the romance of the sea and did not want to know where they were going until they were on their way there.

Throughout the afternoon, there had been no wind other than that created by the *Slecome Bay*'s passage through the calm sea that moved only very lazily to a slight swell; her wake stretched straight and was discernible until distance merged it into the surrounding water.

By dark, visibility was considerably reduced and when the Mate handed the watch over to the Third, he happily forecast a thickening fog. There are none so cheerfully pessimistic as an officer leaving his relief to face problems that might lie ahead.

17

Judging visibility at night was difficult and the Third was on his first trip since gaining his Second Mate's ticket. He stood on the wing of the bridge and, as he stared out, tried to make up his mind whether or not to call the Captain. One minute the twirling wisps of dirty cotton wool seemed to be thickening, the next they did not. He went into the wheelhouse and past the man at the helm to the radar display that was aft of the flag locker. The screen showed a vessel almost abeam to starboard at four miles' range. Out on the wing, he had not seen her lights – the fog had thickened very considerably. He returned to the starboard wing and checked that the lights really were not visible, unplugged the voice pipe – the Captain suffered many foibles, one of which was his hatred of telephones – and blew. When there was a curt "Yes?", he reported that visibility had suddenly closed.

"Ring stand-by."

He gripped both handles of the engine-room telegraph and swung them round to full astern, then back up to stand-by. Seconds later, the jangle of bells and the inner pointer signalled the engine room's acceptance of the order.

The Captain arrived on the bridge. A small man, with very broad shoulders, his normal expression suggested he suffered from severe constipation. He stepped out on to the starboard wing and let his eyes become used to the darkness. "Why didn't you call me earlier?" he suddenly snapped.

"It's only just thickened, sir."

He made a sound that indicated contemptuous disbelief. "Have you set a look-out on the fo'c'sle head?"

"No, sir."

"Why not?"

"Like I said, sir, it's only just—"

"Have you started the foghorn?"

Since nothing could have been more obvious than that he had not, the Third remained silent.

"Why do I have to check every bloody thing on the

ship?" the Captain asked the night. "Have you looked at the radar?"

"Yes, sir," the Third answered, grateful for the chance to prove he was not totally incompetent. "There's one ship out on our starboard beam at four miles."

"Are you going to start the foghorn and set the look-out or do you expect me to do that for you?"

The Third moved until he could swing down the short lever which started the automatic foghorn; there was a deep, mournful blast of sound. He went into the wheelhouse and pressed the call button on the after bulkhead to summon the standby. The foghorn sounded again and, having too much imagination for the job, he momentarily thought it sounded like a wounded bull elephant.

He checked the radar screen, returned to the wing. "I've called the standby, sir, and when he comes I'll tell him to post a lookout. The ship to starboard is now aft of our beam and there are no other echoes."

The Captain didn't bother to acknowledge the report.

Cain hurried into the room. "I've been trying to break free for the last hour. If words were valuable, the Super would be a rich man." He stared at the deed box on his desk. "The money's in that?"

"All there, Sarge," Keen replied, "together with the signet ring. This booklet was in it as well." He opened the lid of the box and dropped the report onto the money.

"Let's move, then."

He picked up the deed box, followed Cain along the short stretch of the corridor to the detective inspector's room.

Drew stood. "We'll go down to the conference room. It'll be easier to make the count on a table that size." A tall, well-built man, his appearance was hawkish thanks to an aquiline nose, a mouth that even in repose suggested a degree of impatience, and a very determined chin. His manner was sharp and he seldom made an effort to hide his annoyance if he had to deal with someone of slow intelligence, or his anger when faced with incompetence. Those who worked under him respected his ability, but resented his refusal to accept that occasionally circumstances would prevent a man completing what he'd set out to do. Few doubted that spurred on by ambition he would make high rank, or that when he did, he would become an even more demanding superior. He did not immediately move from behind the desk. "Is there any later news on the victim?"

"No, sir," Keen replied.

"Have you been able to contact a relative?"

"I've identified someone who is probably his niece, but haven't yet spoken to her."

"It would be an idea to do so."

Cain, for once standing up for a DC, said: "I told Mike to forget everything else and come straight here with the money."

"Then see the lady's contacted as soon as we've finished . . . Do we have a lead on the car?"

Keen answered. "PC Gains had a word with the eyewitness, Miss Logan, and she told him—"

"Haven't you questioned her?"

"I reckoned the first thing was to identify a relative or close friend. We had to break into the house to try to find a useful name and that's when the money turned up and—"

"What did Miss Logan tell PC Gains?"

"She only saw the car at a distance and after the incident. She couldn't say anything more about it other than that it was a light grey."

"Hopefully, after the sense of shock has worn off, she'll be a little more helpful than that . . . Right, let's go."

Drew, a keep-fit enthusiast, came briskly around his desk, crossed the room and led the way down the three flights of stairs, scorning the lift, much to Cain's breathless annoyance.

The conference room overlooked a road on the far side of which was a Georgian rectory, half hidden behind a luxuriant horse chestnut tree. The oblong table, lightly scarred by many years' use, seated sixteen people.

Drew said: "We will each make a full count." He stopped, spoke to Keen. "I presume you already have signed totals?"

"Yes, sir. PC Gains and I differed by eighty pounds on our first count, agreed on our second."

"You did not make a third one?"

"No, sir."

"You should have done."

Quite! "I thought it more important to get the money to safety."

"And less onerous . . . Empty out the box."

Keen opened the lid, picked up the booklet. "This and a signet ring were also in the box."

"Where's the ring?"

"Under the notes."

"What's the booklet?"

"The report of an official inquiry into a collision at sea."

"Riveting reading."

Drew seldom spoke lightly and his listeners were uncertain whether or not be had intended ironic humour.

Keen emptied the contents of the box onto the table. The signet ring jerkily rolled free of the notes.

"Pass me that," Drew said. When it was handed to him, he held it up and visually examined it. "A bit of an arty-farty setting." He liked things to be austere; he did not approve of signet rings for men. "We'll need to know if the stone's a genuine ruby and roughly what it's worth, so get a jeweller's estimate. Check the Stolen Property lists to see if this is on any of 'em." He sat, put the ring down on the table to his right. "Divide the bundles of notes into three. After counting one bundle, pass it to your left."

They counted. Distantly heard, the clock of the parish church chimed the hour as Cain added up his totals.

"Well?" Drew said impatiently.

"One hundred and sixty-two thousand, seven hundred and fifty pounds, sir."

Drew turned to Keen. "And you?"

"The same. And that agrees with the second count that PC Gains and I made."

"Since it agrees with my figure, we will take it as accurate . . . You've brought up a Property Inward form and sealing tape?"

How the hell, Keen thought, was he supposed to have done that when they'd come straight from the DI's room? But one did not ask a senior officer to be reasonable.

He took a lift down to the ground floor. He got the key from the duty sergeant and signed for it, went through the charge room and along a corridor which smelt of stale humanity, unlocked the door of the property room and entered, signed the Movement Book and recorded the reason for his visit, collected two inward forms and a half-used roll of tape, signed for them; he returned the key to the duty sergeant and entered the time of doing this and then, satisfied he had fulfilled all the demands of police bureaucracy, returned upstairs by lift.

Cain had returned the money to the deed box. Keen wound tape around the box lengthwise and sideways. Then, in reverse order of seniority, each of them signed, making certain he did so at a point where tape crossed tape. Keen made out the Property Inward form, passed it across.

"You've left out the booklet," Drew said sharply.

"I didn't think . . ."

"Obviously."

Some people had to work at being obnoxious, Drew did not. Keen took back the form and added the booklet.

Drew stood, crossed to the window and looked out. He said, not turning back: "Have you any hint as to why there was so much cash in the house?"

"No, sir," Keen replied.

"What about bank accounts?"

"There's not been time to check out that possibility."

"An efficient officer makes time."

"But if that sort of money came in legitimately, wouldn't he have left it in the bank for security or invested it?"

"Any reasonable man would, but your job should have taught you that for every two reasonable men there's one unreasonable one. There are still people out there who keep their cash under their mattresses."

"Wouldn't a hundred and sixty thousand in notes make sleeping uncomfortable?"

"Check for bank accounts," Drew snapped.

"Yes, sir."

"Do we know Noyes?"

Translated, does he have a criminal record? "As far as I can tell, no, but I haven't had time to consult Records."

"Failing any indications of legitimacy, it's difficult to think what other than drug money could produce this much cash."

"There was nothing in the house to suggest drugs. But . . ."

"Well?"

"There was something odd about the accident."

Drew turned round, stared at Keen, the expression in his dark brown eyes sharp. "What exactly?"

"Miss Logan said the car was travelling west. Noyes was walking towards the crossroads so he was going east. The car was right over on its wrong side of the road when it hit him. Normally, that would mean the driver had lost control, but there are no skid or panic-braking marks on the road. What's more, Noyes would have been in view of the driver for several hundred yards if the car came straight across the crossroads and for perhaps three hundred if it had turned in from right or left – plenty of distance to realise the danger and react."

"What conclusion do you draw?"

"None, sir." For Drew, conclusions had to be backed by facts. "But remembering all this money, there does seem to be the possibility he was deliberately run down."

Drew stared at Keen for several seconds, then abruptly spoke to Cain. "We need far more information, especially about Noyes and his financial affairs. See to it." He walked briskly across to the door, left.

Cain said: "Get this box down to Property, check out the ring on the Stolen Property lists, ask a jeweller to value it; speak to banks and building societies; get a line on the niece . . ."

"I've enough on my plate already to keep two of me on continuous overtime."

Cain ignored that. "Speak to Miss Logan. Have you any idea what sort of a woman she is?"

"Can't say more than that she's got a lot of years behind her and looks sharpish."

"See if you can get more sense out of her beyond the car being light grey. Have a search for anyone else who saw or heard anything. And take this money down to Property so it's someone else's problem. My digestion will be all to hell until I know that's done."

Keen reached out to pick up the deed box, then withdrew his hands. "There's something has me wondering, Sarge. This box was hidden away because of the money and the signet ring – but why did he bother to add the report?"

"Forgotten it was in the box."

"It was on top of the notes . . . Why keep the report of a collision at sea that happened not far short of forty years ago?"

"Tell me."

"Maybe it was in the safest place he could find because somehow it has a direct connection with what happened today."

"No one's going to accuse you of a lack of imagination," was Cain's morose comment.

"So it could be a good idea to read right through it?"

"So long as you do it in your own time."

24

Three

B arrat looked up from his desk as Keen entered the CID
general room. "Jean wants to know if you and Anne can
come for lunch at the weekend, Saturday or Sunday, doesn't
matter which?"

"I'm not certain. Can I let you know?"

"Sure. Just a light meal and a jar, or two."

He sat at his desk. Barrat, a relatively small man with a face
that marked his tenacity, would have been understandingly
sorry to hear that he and Anne had proved to be one more
couple unable to survive the exigencies of the police force and
had split up. But he found himself unable to admit the fact.
Perhaps this was because he knew Anne had seen his ready
acceptance of the canteen culture, the sense of very strong
loyalty to one's fellow officers, the coarse, sexist attitudes, as a
rejection of herself . . .

"Rolf said you've been out on a fatality?"

He described events, happy to keep his thoughts away from
home. "And right now, I'd better get on to the hospital and
find out how the poor sod is."

Barrat stood, searched for, and found on another desk the
Duty Book. He said, as he wrote: "I've got to get out to
Akstone for the third time to try to take a witness statement
from a pensioner. First he was on some seaside outing, then it
was a trip to a matinée in London. These days, it's the
toothless oldies who have all the fun, not us youngsters."
He closed the Duty Book, stood. "Give us a ring at home

about the meal." He threaded a way between the desks to the doorway, left.

Jean Barrat and Anne had been good friends from the day they'd met at work and discovered they were both married to policemen. Theirs was a friendship of differences. Jean had a light-hearted approach to life, Anne a more serious one; Jean let the future look after itself, Anne tried to plan it; Jean would dismiss a problem if she couldn't immediately deal with it, Anne would mull over it, even if she found it more and more intractable by doing so. Ironically, their children reversed these characteristics. Jean's son had the gravitas of an elder statesman who took himself too seriously, Judy lived a life of bubbles and laughter . . . That was, she had before Anne had dragged her away . . .

He collected the telephone from two desks away, checked the number of the hospital, dialled. Identifying himself as CID ensured he quickly spoke to someone who could give him the facts. Noyes was now in the operating theatre and had been for some considerable time; he had suffered a crushed pelvis and severe internal injuries, the full extent of which was not yet certain. Officially, it was impossible to give a prognosis; unofficially, it would be something of a miracle if he lived.

He thanked the other, rang off. If some of the questions surrounding the accident were to be answered, it seemed unlikely it would be Noyes who did the answering.

He opened the Xmas card he had found in the drawer of Noyes's bedside table and checked the address. He asked Directory Enquiries to give him the number of 24 Sibton Avenue, Richly Cross. After a long wait, a bad-tempered lecture about the extra work involved when a caller didn't know all the facts, he was given a name – Ellis – and a number. He dialled this.

His call was answered after several rings. "Mrs Laura Ellis?"

"Yes."

"My name's Detective Constable Keen, Clunford CID—"

She interrupted him, her voice high. "What's happened to Sandra?"

He judged Sandra to be a daughter. "As far as I know, she's perfectly all right. The reason for this call is to ask if you have an uncle by the name of Reginald Noyes?"

"Yes. Why?"

"I'm very sorry to have to tell you that he's had an accident and is in hospital."

"I see."

He was surprised by her apparent lack of emotion. "He was hit by a car when walking along the road near his home and he's suffered fairly severe injuries, the extent of which isn't yet certain." He waited for a comment; there was none. "I expect you'd like the telephone number of the hospital so that you can get in touch?"

"I suppose so."

He gave her the number. "Are you Mr Noyes's next of kin?"

"As far as I know, he hasn't any other relatives."

"Then I need to have a chat with you."

"Why?"

"The car didn't stop and so we have to try to identify the driver."

"I don't understand how I can possibly help you do that."

"I know it must sound like a very long shot, but experience shows that sometimes long shots succeed. He may have told you about . . ."

"He's told me nothing."

She'd spoken with considerable force. Why? "Nevertheless, I do need to speak to you. Perhaps you could call in here, at the police station, on your way to or from the hospital?"

"I can't say when I can visit him. I've only recently moved and don't know of someone who would come and babysit."

"Then it sounds as if it would be easier for you if I drove over to your house. If we could fix a time now?"

27

"I can't. I don't know what's happening."

"I'll phone again to see if it will be easier then to arrange something." He said goodbye. A strange conversation, but at least he could, judging by her attitude, be assured that he'd escaped the worst job for any policeman, bringing tragedy to someone's life.

He looked at his watch. There was time to have a jeweller's opinion of the signet ring before he went to a pub where the landlord had his ear very close to the ground.

The small jeweller's at the back of the High Street was dying a lingering death. The window display was dull; the interior might not have altered in fifty years and seemed to be carrying the scent of aged dust even though it was clean. At seventy-one, with heavily lined face, pouched eyes, and wearing a shabby suit, Robert Culrose appeared to be as moribund as his shop yet under that tired, defeated exterior, he possessed a passion for his work, a knowledge of jewellery that was far more extensive than his trade had ever warranted, and the fixed opinion that for every woman there were only certain jewels which would complement.

He had a sense of humour that most found puerile. "Dr Holmes, I presume?"

"According to my DI, more Watson on one of his off days."

"You are referring to Mr Drew? He was guest speaker at one of our little lunches and he struck me as a man of many sharp and strong opinions."

"But give the devil his due, they're more often right than wrong."

"Then would he were a member of the government."

"Nothing would get me emigrating quicker! . . . I've come for some help."

"Dear me! I was hoping you were going to buy the sapphire ring I have been guarding for several years, waiting for the right person to wear it."

On more than one occasion, Culrose had said to Anne that she should wear sapphires . . . Could he, Keen thought with sudden bitterness, go nowhere, do nothing, without being reminded of her? "I'd be grateful if you'd look at a signet ring and tell me anything you can about it." He brought an envelope out of his pocket, opened this and allowed the ring to roll out onto the glass-topped counter.

Culrose hastily produced a square of black velvet. "More care, if you please. Cats, women and jewellery should be caressed, not handled." He picked up the ring, held it up in front of his eyes as he slowly turned it round. "Almost certainly made by Pierce. A man who is christened Cuthbert is hardly likely to understand that far from being flamboyant, jewellery should be restrained." He brought a jeweller's eye-glass out of his pocket and put this up to his right eye. After a moment, he said, with satisfaction: "Indeed, Cuthbert! Made in nineteen hundred and eight when his popularity was high, the Edwardian era being an ostentatious one. After his death, his work rightly fell out of favour, but there was a resurgence in its popularity in the fifties, perhaps because it provided a contrast to the austerity the then government delighted on imposing on us, if not themselves. Almost certainly, the initials were added at a much later date."

"Initials?"

"You have not noticed them? That is hardly to be wondered at since they are only just visible under the eyeglass. In contrast to the ring, they show the work of a true craftsman."

"What are they?"

"I'll need stronger magnification to be certain." He put the eyeglass down on the counter, opened a drawer and brought out a large magnifying glass. Holding the ring under an adjustable light, he studied it for a while. "R and B, entwined."

"No throbbing heart?"

"Don't mock the trappings of sentiment. They help to make life bearable."

29

"Is that a genuine ruby?"

"Pierce would be outraged by the question. His boast was that the best was only just good enough for him. It will be of the finest quality; from Burma, naturally."

"So what's the ring worth?"

"More than its intrinsic value because Pierce's work has remained in vogue and is now referred to as highly collectable. We live in a strange age in which values have been turned upside down – the less genuinely valuable to mankind a man's work, the more he is likely to be paid. There was a sale recently at which one of his most elaborate pieces fetched twice its estimated value . . . This will be worth several thousand pounds."

Keen whistled.

South Clunford had become the least salubrious part of the town; the Dirty Duck stood on the corner of a Y-junction.

Keen asked for a half-pint of bitter. When the barmaid served him, he told her he'd like a word with Bert. She nodded, but said nothing. As he drank, he automatically studied those around him – detective or criminal was liable to disclose his calling to a knowledgeable observer by his constant surveillance of others. One face seemed familiar, but he couldn't put a name to it: he filed a mental picture.

Ogden walked along the bar to stand opposite him. "You want something?" he asked in a neutral tone, not welcoming the meeting, yet at the same time not resentful of it. Their relationship was difficult to define. He would pass on information that came his way, but only some of it; self-interest meant it paid him to be friendly with the police, but also not to be known to his customers and their friends as a loose-lipped informer.

"Does the name Reg Noyes ring any bells?" Keen asked.

"Should it?"

"He could be working the hard stuff."

"I've heard nothing."

That could well be the truth. Ogden had reason to hate the drug trade – a niece of whom he'd been very fond had died from an overdose of heroin because the bag she'd bought had not been cut nearly as heavily as she'd expected. "If any news comes your way, I'd like to hear it."

Ogden nodded.

Keen drained his glass and asked for another half-pint.

Four

B ecause of other work – in particular, investigating a
warehouse robbery – it was after six before Keen drove
out to Kingsholte and parked in front of Miss Logan's
bungalow. He climbed out of the car and looked along the
road. Difficult now to place amongst the countryside peace the
agony of the morning . . .

The bungalow had the graceless lines of the thirties. He
opened the wrought-iron gate and walked up the gravel path,
past a small lawn and three flowerbeds in which not a weed
was visible. The knocker on the front door was in the shape of
a horse's head.

Miss Logan opened the door. A small woman, with a
hoppity, birdlike manner, she saw no reason to be concerned
about what other people's opinions of her appearance might
be – her luxuriant black hair was tied in an unbecoming bun,
she wore no make-up, glasses hung from her neck on a frayed
cord, and her dress, in a sad brown, could in an earlier age well
have been worn by an almshouse matron. Her manner was
friendly. In her day, one had respect for the forces of law and
order.

"Please come in . . . No, James, don't bother the gentleman." This last addressed to a Yorkshire terrier that had a red
bow around its neck.

"Don't worry," he said, "I like dogs." He bent down to pat
James and nearly had his hand bitten as a result.

"He sometimes becomes a little excited."

33

James was behaving as if a sharp nip to an ankle was good, clean fun. He should, he thought, have said that he liked some dogs. "Sorry to bother you, but I need to ask a few questions about this morning."

"So distressing to find him in such pain and to be unable to do anything to alleviate that."

She had spoken with sincerity. A woman, he judged, whose appearance and manner belied her inner strength and emotional resolution. "When you phoned emergency, you probably helped him more than anything else you could have done."

"I should like to think that. How is the poor man?"

"We haven't had a recent report. The last we heard, he was in the operating theatre. There may be problems because of internal injuries."

"One must hope they are not too serious. Shall we go through to the sitting room?"

As he moved, James growled and curled his lips.

"Be quiet, James," she said. "Mr Keen is a friend."

And mark that well, you little sod! he thought.

The sitting room had chintz curtains, flowery covers on the chairs, a display cabinet filled with mementoes rather than *objets d'art*, a mantelpiece crowded with photographs, a heavily framed portrait in oils of a stern man in robes who stared out at a world he condemned . . .

"Do sit down. And then tell me what it is you want to ask me."

He sat as she settled in the second armchair. "In part, it's what can you tell us about Mr Noyes."

"I thought I'd explained to the constable this morning that although he has now lived here for a few years, I hardly know him. He . . . I hesitate to criticise someone who is badly injured, but the fact is, I have taken care not to become friendly with him although he has frequently made it obvious that he would welcome a closer acquaintance."

Her speech had as many echoes of the past as did her manners and appearance.

"Would that be because of the type of man he is?"

She considered the question for a while before answering. "When he moved here with his wife – she died not long afterwards – I naturally asked them along for a drink as one does with new neighbours. It was not a happy visit. I find coarseness in speech and behaviour very unwelcome."

"So that was almost the last you saw of them?"

"His wife became very ill and quite unable to receive visitors. After she died, it was obvious that any restraint she had been able to exercise over his behaviour was now totally gone."

"You're referring to visitors he had to stay?"

"I am indeed."

"Would you think they were . . ." He hesitated, uncertain how to word the question.

"They clearly were prostitutes."

He should have given her credit for a straight tongue. "Would you say he was a wealthy man?"

"That was the impression he was constantly trying to give."

"In what way?"

"After his wife died, he frequently went away for weeks at a time and when he returned he invariably made a point of speaking to me when I was in the garden – however obvious I made it that this was unwelcome – and telling me he'd been on a luxury cruise and how much he'd paid for a deluxe cabin or a suite. As my dear father said, a gentleman only discusses money with a bank manager. Of course, he had enough sense not to try to make out he was a gentleman. Indeed, there were occasions when it seemed he wished to do the exact opposite. He once told me that he went on the cruises because he gained such pleasure from making a nuisance of himself and getting his own back. Do you not find that extraordinary behaviour?"

"Very much so. Did he ever say anything that helped to explain it?"

"No. And I certainly didn't encourage him by showing the slightest interest . . . And now you can do some explaining. Why are you asking all these questions?"

"We have to try and identify the car."

"And how will it help you do that to know what kind of a man he is?"

"It's always best to get a rounded picture of everyone."

"Fiddlesticks!"

She had spoken in a tone that prompted James to move directly in front of Keen and growl. Keen drew his feet closer to the chair.

"I assume that a man of his character would have an unsavoury past. Presumably, you are trying to confirm such presumption?"

"As I said, Miss Logan, all I'm trying to do is identify the car." He quickly changed the course of the conversation. "I understand that this morning you were outside when the incident occurred?"

"I do not sleep very well and if the weather's fine I get up early and go out and garden. There is quite a lot of land at the back and I grow vegetables. Now that all the greengrocers have vanished and one has perforce to resort to supermarkets, it is impossible to buy beans which aren't coarse or tomatoes that have any taste."

He imagined her digging, hoeing, weeding, watering, showing an energy someone half her age might well envy. "Were you in the vegetable garden before the time of the accident?"

"I had been in the front garden for quite some time; probably more than half an hour."

"During that time, did you notice anyone or anything unusual?"

"I'm not sure I understand exactly what you mean."

"There's usually a pattern to life in the countryside. One

sees people one expects to see, doing things one expects them to do. So a stranger, or someone one knows doing something one has never seen him do before, becomes unusual."

"You seem to have an outdated picture of the countryside," she observed with amusement. "These days, there's considerable traffic along this road and it's impossible to know to whom the cars belong. As for pedestrians, many are strangers, seen once and never again. According to the postman, who is garrulous, the woods are a favoured place for young couples to visit. To judge by their behaviour when they pass here, he could well be correct."

"Did you notice a car which went past more than once some short time before the accident?"

"The only car I noted is the one I saw parked by Bunyon's Field."

"Was there a reason for noticing that?"

"Bunyon's Field belongs to Mr Feldrun, who is a pleasant man, but a boor, because every time he meets me he complains endlessly about the people who roam in his field and damage the crops. When I saw the car, I wondered whether someone from it was walking over the corn. I keep telling him he ought to use a bull to stop all the trespassing."

"If that were his motive, it would be illegal."

"I dare say. All private rights are being abolished. As my dear father used to say, when a politician calls upon the virtues of equality, he's supping with the devil."

"Have you any idea how long the car was parked there?"

"Perhaps a quarter of an hour."

"Did you see it drive off?"

"I was about to pick up some dead leaves when it came past. Being driven far too quickly."

"Going in which direction?"

"Towards the crossroads."

"How long before the accident was that?"

"Very few minutes."

"Can you say what make of car it was?"

"As I explained to the constable this morning, these days I cannot tell one make from another. My dear father always bought Rovers – good, but not ostentatious, he said – and you could never mistake one. But these days, they look like any other car."

"What colour was it?"

"Light grey."

"Was it a saloon?"

"It was what we used to call a shooting brake, but I'm told they have a different name these days."

"Estate cars . . . What happened after it had passed here?"

"I've no idea. I wasn't watching it."

"I meant, as far as you were concerned. I believe you saw Mr Noyes walking towards the crossroads?"

"That is correct. Then I picked up the leaves and carried them to the dustbin, returned for some rose prunings."

"Were those the ones you were putting in the dustbin when you heard the accident?"

"They were."

"So what did you do next?"

"I dropped the cuttings and hurried back to the front garden and saw Mr Noyes lying on the verge on the opposite side of the road."

"Was there a car in sight?"

"There was one, driving up to the corner at a ridiculous speed."

"On which side of the road?"

"On the left, of course. The government may have destroyed so much that is British with their beastly metrication, but at least they still allow us to drive on the correct side of the road."

"You told PC Gains the car was a light grey?"

"I did."

"Was it a shooting brake?"

She did not answer for several seconds. "I . . . I think so."

"And you tried to read the number plate, but failed?"

"I have these for distance." She tapped the glasses which hung from her neck. "But in the rush of events, I didn't put them on."

"Very understandable."

"Very stupid!"

He momentarily thought she was criticising his attempt to comfort, realised she was castigating herself. "Do you reckon the car which had been parked by Bunyon's Field and the car which you saw driving away after the accident could have been the same one?"

"Quite possibly. But I cannot say for certain."

Drew did not seem to place much credence in his suggestion that the incident might not have been an accident, but an attempt to murder; Cain dismissed the possibility. But until the source of all that money was identified and found to be irrelevant to the accident, there surely was reason to keep it in mind? . . . Assume the two cars were one and the same. The driver had parked by the field in order to see when Noyes left his house, as he did every day, to walk to the village to collect the paper. Having previously established distances and times, the driver knew how far and fast to drive before returning to meet Noyes head-on and smash him to the ground . . . "That seems to be everything, Miss Logan. Thank you for all your help." He stood.

James growled.

"Usually James only behaves like this towards people he doesn't trust," she said.

Even by the time he was back in his car, he couldn't decide whether she had been expressing surprise or wondering if James's aggressive attitude might be justified. Back in the CID general room at divisional HQ, he telephoned the hospital. Noyes had died; his internal injuries had proved to be far more severe than previously judged.

Murder or accident? In his mind, he flipped a coin. Then could not decide whether it came down heads or tails.

Five

T hey had bought No.5 Craythorne Road one year after their marriage, a year before Judy was born. Anne, who had always declared herself to be a modern woman, had surprised him by demanding he carry her over the threshold. How else to guarantee a long and happy marriage? How else? As he drove into the garage to the left of the semi-detached house, he remembered bitterly how she'd giggled as he picked her up and then said something which had nearly made him drop her from surprise – she had always been such a nicely spoken, modest young lady . . .

He unlocked the front door and went into the hall. No sounds from the front room because Judy was not in there, watching a children's programme on television; no succulent smells wafting out of the kitchen because Anne was not in there, cooking supper. Only silence.

He went through the deserted kitchen and into the larder. When their marriage had begun to shake, she'd repeatedly accused him of drinking too much. An intelligent woman, yet she'd been unable to understand that the easiest way of relaxing and shedding stress was to have a drink or two with the lads. Had she wanted him home when he was like a rubber band stretched to snapping point? He poured himself a gin and tonic, carried the glass through to the sitting room, switched on the television. Her favourite programme was showing. He switched off the set. He finished his drink, went through to the larder and poured himself another, returned. He picked up the

Daily Mail, which she must have put on the coffee table before she left. Soon, he dropped the paper onto the floor. Who really cared if yet another politician had been caught with his hand in the cookie jar, workers were threatening to strike, a woman of sixty-two had had a baby, or World War Three was prophesied by a mystic from Maharashtra who claimed to have named the days of the outbreaks of the wars in Korea, Vietnam, Iraq . . . He drained his glass and thought about refilling it, decided he had had enough. He returned to the larder and poured himself a third gin and tonic.

In the hall, he stopped and stared at the phone on the table by the stairs. Suppose he asked Anne to return, promised to spend much less time with the lads . . . Goddamit, why should he have to make all the moves? Wasn't the present situation more her fault than his because she deliberately did not understand? If she desperately wanted to get away from him, was so selfish she didn't care about Judy's future, so be it. He wasn't going to get down on his knees . . . He picked up the receiver, dialled the number.

"Eckinton six one five four," Fay said.

He liked Fay, envied Ifor because of the lifestyle he could provide her with. Two Mercedes, a big one for her, a bigger one for himself. Conspicuous bloody consumption! Social bloody divisiveness . . .

"Are you going to tell me who you are or is the deep breathing about to start?"

"Mike."

"*Quelle* wonderful *surprise!*"

"Is it?"

"You need to ask?"

"Is Anne there?"

"She's patiently listening to Ifor telling her for the umpteenth time how he almost holed out in one the other day. I've never told him this, but I think he was probably aiming for a different hole."

"I want to speak to her."

"Sweetie, I know you're a man and so don't welcome advice, but do try to tread like Icarus."

"Who?"

"He walked on eggshells."

"Aren't you thinking of Agag?"

"I believe I am. What a clever man you are!"

"I suppose she's been moaning about me?"

"Your darling wife is the soul of loyal discretion. So much so, I still haven't been given even a whisper about why she's staying here . . . Hang on and I'll get her. But remember, tread like . . . Who?"

"Agag."

"What it is to have a memory."

He waited.

"Yes?" Anne said.

Her tone was sharp. He forgot the need to tread carefully. "I want you to come back here."

"Suppose that for once I prefer to do what I want?"

"What about Judy?"

"She's tucked up in bed and fast asleep."

"That's not what I meant."

"It isn't?"

"Breaking up the family is the worst possible thing for her."

"Worse than repeatedly allowing her to understand that her father would far rather spend time drinking than read to her as promised?"

"That's only happened the once."

"It's never occurred to you, has it, that every time you could return to say goodnight before she goes to sleep, but don't, you're breaking your promise as a father?"

"That's ridiculous . . ." He tried to control his emotions. "Come on back and we'll sort things out."

"Until you can understand that what I said isn't ridiculous, I'm not returning."

"Why not? I suppose you think . . ."

"That you've been drinking."

"I've had one, yes."

"Multiply that."

"I'm not tight, if that's what you're snidely trying to make out. Why won't you tell me what's really bugging you?"

"Since the beginning of the year, have you once stopped to think what I'd like to do rather than what you want to do?"

"You like going out for a meal. I've taken you as often as we could afford."

"When was the last time?"

"Two, three weeks ago."

"Over three months."

About to deny that possibility angrily, he remembered they'd gone to the Italian restaurant in Goodge Street and that had been closed for renovation for several weeks. "I was hoping we'd go this weekend."

"You're good at hoping, not very good at doing. There's no point in going on like this. Goodnight, Mike."

"Hang on . . ." The line went dead.

He swore. He returned to the sitting room, slumped down in an armchair. She accused him of neglecting her. That seemed to be the favourite complaint of wives. Hew had recently said his wife was moaning like hell because he was leaving her to spend most of her waking hours, and many of her sleeping ones, on her own. Work, and a man was blamed for not being at home; stay at home and he was branded a layabout . . .

He was hungry. He went through to the kitchen and opened the refrigerator. On one of the shelves was a plate of mince, covered with cling film, waiting to be turned into shepherd's pie. But if Anne wasn't there, it would stay as mince because he knew as much about cooking as she did about team bonding. Perhaps she had left it as a subtle two fingers to him. Women had developed to perfection the art of slipping a dagger into a man . . .

He made a slab-sandwich with Cheddar cheese and pickle,

ate it in the sitting room as he half watched a nature programme on the television. When he'd finished eating, he
decided to turn in, but then checked the time and discovered
it was not yet ten. It was ironic! Anne had left because he was
never at home, yet here he was, sitting around and bored. Life
was endlessly perverse. Noyes had had a hundred and sixty-
two thousand, seven hundred and fifty pounds to spend on
riotous debauchery and so what did life do to him? Killed him.
Or was the driver of the grey car sufficiently independent of
life to carry the blame? . . . One car seen before the fatal
collision, one seen afterwards, both light grey, both possibly
estates; the same car? A very tenuous thread. Yet the finest of
threads could entwine with another, and another, to form a
strong rope . . . If Noyes had been murdered, the odds surely
had to be that the money in the deed box provided either the
direct or the indirect motive? Drugs? Neither of the two
informers he ran, nor the landlord of the Dirty Duck, had
come through to say Noyes's name was known on the streets,
which meant it almost certainly wasn't. If not drugs, what?

He'd said he thought that because the report on the collision
had been kept with the money, it was in some way probably
connected. Since he'd nothing else to do, why not read
through the rest of it and find out if he could be right? Anne
wasn't there moaning he should be talking to her . . .

The booklet was on the table in the hall. He collected it, sat
once more, but did not immediately start reading. When he
and Anne had been engaged, she'd told him that ever since
she'd seen *South Pacific* on the television she'd had the
ambition to travel to a coral island, lie under a coconut tree,
sleep in a palm-thatched hut, and swim in a Prussian-blue sea.
He'd promised to take her to one. Engagement bred an
optimism that marriage soon squashed.

He opened the report and found the point at which he
stopped reading when in the detective sergeant's room.

* * *

By midnight, the fog had thickened into rolls of grey opaqueness. The air smelled damp and moisture had gathered in drops on the standard and gyro binnacles on the monkey island and on the telegraphs on the wings. The sea was sullenly calm and the swell almost gone; as the *Slecome Bay* steamed on, she moved so slightly it was as if the sea were caressing her. At regular intervals, the fog horn sounded its ugly blast.

The Second Mate climbed the companionway and entered the chartroom, crossed to the table and noted the last marked position, determined by Decca Navigator, on the opened chart, skimmed through the eight to twelve entry in the rough logbook. In the wheelhouse, he studied the radar screen – one blip on the port wing, one astern, both several miles distant. He carried on through to the port wing, knowing that the Captain – ever the traditionalist – always paced the starboard wing unless conditions were less bearable than on the port one.

"You're late," the Third said.

"Seven minutes only," he replied equably.

"The Old Man wants a radar report every ten minutes."

"Does he know what to do with it when he gets it?"

"Course zero six five, engines on half speed. I'm off." He left.

The Second crossed through the wheelhouse to the starboard wing. The Captain, who'd been pacing athwartships, came to a halt. "Only two echoes on the screen, sir, both well clear."

The Captain grunted an acknowledgement.

The Second returned into the wheelhouse and used a torch to help himself to the jam sandwiches – stale – and the coffee – ground acorns? – which the standby had brought up.

He checked the radar again, went out on to the port wing and began to pace fore and aft. It was threatening to be a poor-value trip. Only one passenger worth the effort. She wasn't young, she wasn't beautiful, but she did possess an air of liking the questions, knowing the answers, and having the

sense not to tell her husband too many details about the trip
when she arrived home. The odd thing was, he wasn't making
the progress he expected. She spent time with him during the
day, but so far had refused a drink in his cabin at night. Still, it
could only be a question of time . . .

0243 hours.

A fresh blip came up on the radar screen, bearing ten
degrees to port, distance about nine miles, to join the other
three echoes on the starboard bow which formed a rough
triangle, suggesting they could be fishing vessels.

The Captain stood in front of the screen, his gnarled
features set in morose lines. As he watched, the distance of
the blip on their port bow shortened, but the bearing did not
alter. It seemed the oncoming vessel was on a converging
collision course. "Starboard five degrees."

"Starboard five," repeated the helmsman as he moved the
wheel two spokes to starboard. He judged the swing of the
bows, returned the wheel amidships. "Steering zero seven
zero, sir."

The Captain mentally judged whether to reduce speed. If
the other vessel were on a reciprocal course, it would be better
not to do so because then she would have more room; thanks
to the alteration of course, she should pass on the port side
without any problem.

The bearing remained steady. The distance shortened to five
miles. The Captain gave the order to alter five degrees to
starboard, went out on to the port wing. "Can you hear any
fog signal, Second?"

"No, sir."

He returned to the radar. The distance was down to three
miles on the same bearing. He cursed the men on the other
ship as fools, considered altering course to port to let them
pass to starboard, decided that as they were so firmly on the
Slecome Bay's port bow, suddenly swinging to port might

47

confuse them further than they were already confused. "Starboard ten."

The helmsman repeated the order; a moment later, gave the new heading.

The Captain went out onto the port wing. "Any fog signal yet?"

"No, sir."

A buzzer in the wheelhouse sounded. The Second hurried in, soon returned. "The lookout can hear a faint whistle fine on the port bow, sir."

The Captain rushed back to the radar. The bearing was now eight degrees on the port bow, distance two miles, and as he watched, both bearing and distance decreased rapidly before the echo disappeared. He assumed the oncoming vessel had put her helm hard aport and was now crossing their bows and that the echo had disappeared because of a blind spot. He ran out onto the port wing. There was a whistle a point for'd of their beam. Shocked, he realised the other ship had not gone to port, but was converging; from the sound of the whistle, she would pass astern, but close. It would be wrong to stop engines . . .

The whistle sounded again and was now almost on top of them. "Hard a port," he shouted. He moved to his right, gripped the handles of the telegraphs, swung them both to stop, then right aft to full astern.

The bows of the *Atoka* appeared out of the fog, first uncertain lines that wavered, disappeared, and reformed, then hardened. For those on both bridges, time slowed; on the *Slecome Bay*, the Captain refused to accept that his tens of years at sea could lead to this and the Second backed into the wheelhouse because he always considered himself before anything else.

The *Atoka*'s bows rammed the *Slecome Bay* just aft of midships, thrusting her sideways and slicing into her hull with a piercing screech of metal.

* * *

MR TORRENS GILMORE. In opening this case, counsel for the Minister alleged similar faults against both vessels: proceeding at an immoderate speed in fog contrary to Article 16 (a) of the Collision Regulations. Having had ample warning by radar of the presence of the other vessel, not taking steps to avoid a close quarters situation or taking off the vessel's way. Having heard the fog signal of a vessel for'd of the beam, failing to stop engines in accordance with Article 16 (b). On faulty and incomplete information, believing the other vessel was on a reciprocal course and would pass clear.

There can be no doubt that both vessels were proceeding at too great a speed in dense fog, and doing so because of reliance on radar; but in neither case were the radar readings plotted and therefore no true appreciation of the situation was ascertained. These faults are sufficiently serious to force the Court, despite the excellent records of both captains, to suspend their certificates for twelve months.

Are there any applications?

Counsel for both masters asked that their clients be granted a certificate in the meantime. This was agreed to.

Keen stared down at the report. The two masters had had their certificates suspended and then each had been granted a certificate. He could only presume that what was granted enabled each to hold a position of lesser rank than captain, on the analogy of an inspector being demoted to sergeant. And did the lads enjoy taking the piss out of any unfortunate man to whom that happened!

He yawned, checked the time. After midnight. He stood and, because he had not been gripping the booklet firmly, it slipped out of his hands and fell onto the floor. A newspaper cutting, held between the last page of the report and its cover, half appeared. A check showed there were two cuttings, one very brief, the other covering a full page. He read the short one. It was a marriage announcement from *The Times*; Cedric

Searle had been married to Berenice Ambrose. He opened up the second cutting. Inquest on the death of local resident . . . He yawned again and decided to read about the inquest the next day.

Once in bed, he was very conscious of the empty half and could be certain this emptiness would prevent his sleeping. He was asleep almost as soon as he turned off the light.

Six

A s he put the last two rashers of bacon in the frying pan, Keen found himself making a mental note to remind Anne to buy some more. But if he wanted eggs and bacon for breakfast on Wednesday, he was going to have to buy the bacon. A whole new way of life was opening up before him . . .

He poured out a mugful of coffee, dished the eggs and bacon onto a slice of toast, sat at the small table in a corner of the kitchen. Did he ring Anne that evening, or was it better to forget events of the night before, phone in a day or two after she'd returned from work – he presumed she'd carry on with her part-time job despite the domestic upheaval – and apologise, then confess that in truth he had drunk a little too much, in the hopes that this would help her to start to see sense? Rolf Soper maintained that however annoyed a woman was, if a man offered her a few *mea maxima culpas*, she'd forgive. But judging by his stormy love life, Soper either didn't take his own advice or didn't find it as efficacious as he maintained . . . Best leave things as they were and ring the next day, ostensibly to ask how Judy was, and try to discover how best to play things.

He finished the eggs and bacon, buttered another piece of toast and spread marmalade over it, was about to resume eating when he remembered the cutting he had not read the previous night. He stood, edged his way past the corner of the table, went into the sitting room where he picked up the cutting.

As he ate, he read the report of the inquest, which had been opened previously and then been adjourned, held in January 1964.

The Coroner had first explained to the jury that the purpose of the inquest was to decide on the cause of death of Terrence James Orr, aged twenty-one, employed as a steward on SS *Slecome Bay* . . .

You have told us that death was due to drowning in salt water; that the deceased had previously suffered a fractured leg, severe bruising, and a blow to the skull which would have rendered him unconscious?

I think I said that the blow might well have caused unconsciousness rather than that it did.

You are quite correct, that is what you did say. Is there any way of judging whether he was conscious or unconscious when he drowned?

I do not think one can be certain.

Would you care to give an opinion?

Provided it is accepted as no more than an opinion; that I may well be wrong.

What is your opinion?

That the deceased was unconscious when he landed in the sea and that he inhaled water and drowned without regaining consciousness.

You said that the injury to his head was caused by something solid, probably round and of a relatively narrow diameter?

As far as I could judge.

It might well have been a ship's stanchion?

Yes.

The force of the collision with the *Atoka* clearly threw him off balance with sufficient force to cause the broken leg and severe bruising; it is therefore reasonable to suppose that he fell against a stanchion?

With the proviso that he must have struck it with such force that I would have expected further damage to his body than in fact was found. However, I must add that in my experience, one can never be dogmatic about the extent and exact nature of injuries following some traumatic experience.

Are you, in fact, saying that your proviso may well lack justification?

I suppose I am.

You recovered the body of Orr when at sea on the thirteenth of October of last year?

That's right.

Please describe what happened.

There was an object floating on our port bow and we sailed across to find out what it was. As we got near, I could see it was a body so we drew alongside.

One moment, please. Will you tell us whether the body was clothed when you sighted it in the water?

It didn't have nothing on it.

The body was quite naked?

Yes.

Was there any clothing floating in the water nearby?

I didn't see none.

With the air temperature being what it was, would you have expected someone on a ship to walk around on deck in a state of nudity?

CORONER. Is this important?

Sir, for the force of the collision to topple the deceased over the side of the ship, he must have been out on deck and near the rails. We have evidence, taken from the ship's log book, that at midnight the air temperature was only forty-three degrees. In those circumstances, it is difficult to understand why he was walking around on deck when naked.

Could his clothing not have been gradually drawn off him by the action of the sea? He was in the water for over a week.

The evidence is that throughout the ten days, there was either a calm or only a slight sea and very little swell. Would there be enough movement to pluck off the clothing he was wearing; would any movement be sufficient to strip a body completely?

Since his body was naked when recovered, I think we must accept that either this was possible or, for some reason not readily apparent, at the time of the collision he was naked when on deck.

CORONER. Why is this witness being called?

In order to establish whether the deceased might have been expected to be close to the point of collision at the time that it took place, sir.

It seems to me to be a waste of the court's time to establish this. The fact is, he did fall over the side.

With great respect, sir, I think we should establish it.

If you insist.

Will you explain to the court, Mr Windle, how the accommodation on the *Slecome Bay* is laid out.

The captain's flat is on the boat deck, at the for'd end. The passengers' cabins are also on the boat deck, aft of the funnel. The officers' and engineers' cabins are one deck below; the crew's accommodation is on the main deck.

Where was Orr's cabin?

At the for'd end of the crew's accommodation, on the port side.

Is there any deck outside that cabin?

No. Whilst the officers' cabins are a few feet inboard, the crew's and passengers' cabins extend to the hull.

Is it correct, then, to say that to go out on deck, Orr must have gone along a corridor?

He would have had to walk the length of the port alleyway and would have come out on deck just for'd of number four hatch.

How far from such point was it that the bows of the *Atoka* thrust into the *Slecome Bay*?

Approximately forty feet.

So if one assumed Orr was naked at the moment of impact—

CORONER. I don't think we need pursue this point any further.

You shared a cabin with Orr?

Me and Alf likewise. We was three to the cabin.

Were all three of you stewards?

That's right.

On the night of the third of October last year, were you in your cabin?

Later on, I was. Me and some of the lads had a game of poker in the mess and I turned in after that was over.

Can you say at what time you returned to your cabin?

Eleven. Something like that.

Was Orr in the cabin at that time?

No.

Had he been in the mess?

No.

If he wasn't in the mess or in the cabin, can you suggest where he might have been?

Not really.

What does that mean?

Well . . . No.

You have difficulty in deciding whether you can or can't suggest where he might have been?

CORONER. He has answered your question. I must insist that we do not spend any more time on matters which can have very little, or nothing, to do with the purpose of this inquest.

You were the officer on watch?

I was, sir.

Where were you immediately before the collision?

On the port wing.

Please describe what happened.

The bows of the *Atoka* became visible through the fog and it was obvious she was going to hit us because neither helm nor engines could react in time to get us clear. I ran into the wheelhouse to raise the alarm.

Which is where you were when she was struck?

Yes.

How severe would you describe the impact?

If I hadn't grabbed onto the binnacle, I would have been thrown to the deck with considerable force.

So would you say that anyone who was standing and not prepared for the impact would almost certainly have been thrown with sufficient force to suffer injury?

Undoubtedly. And, in fact, I believe a greaser down in the engine room was quite badly injured.

You had no reason to believe someone might have fallen overboard? You heard no cry?

I heard nothing.

The verdict was accidental death. The jury tried to add a rider to the effect that the officers on both ships should have shown greater skill, but the Coroner refused to accept that, saying they could not go beyond their remit and the question of negligence was for others to determine and judge, should it be held that this was necessary.

Seven

Keen had been in the CID general room for only minutes when the "Earts and Narks" phone rang – a separate line which did not go through the main switchboard, it was for incoming personal calls, especially those from informers who did not want to be caught dialling known police numbers. He stood, crossed to the table by the noticeboard, lifted the receiver.

"Is that you, Mister?" a hoarse voice asked.

"Keen by name, keen by nature," he answered, repeating for the umpteenth time the "witticism" because it confirmed his identity.

"You was asking about a new mark on the streets?"

"That's right."

"I ain't heard of one."

"He could be doing business in a small way."

"Don't matter how small, the big 'uns would have him turned into fertiliser."

"Even they must sleep sometimes, so they might have missed. Keep your ears open."

"What about me hands?"

"I'll give 'em something to hold onto the next time we meet."

Keen replaced the receiver. Informers were a fact of police life and without them the clear-up rate might well drop down almost to single figures, but their value to crime detection didn't make them any more acceptable to someone who valued a sense of loyalty.

He went through to the detective sergeant's room to find that empty, but as he turned away, Cain came out of the detective inspector's room, holding the Grid Crime Book in one hand. He passed this to Keen. "You're signed for a burglary in Akers Road, Upington," he said, as he walked around his desk, sat. "That house has been turned over three times in the past six months and there's been more damage than theft because there's not been much to nick, even the first time. So it's likely someone with a grudge or local youths with a perverted sense of humour. Check out the possibilities."

"Will do," Keen said, as he stood in front of the desk. "I've just heard from one of my narks. There's no word on the streets of a new supplier, name of Noyes – or any other name, for that much."

"Your man's not been listening hard enough."

"He's sharp enough to know what's moving before it moves."

"Then ask him what he fancies for the Derby."

"Sarge, if he's heard nothing, there's every chance the money in Noyes's box isn't from drugs. So where did it come from?"

"Tell me."

"I reckon it's somehow tied up with the collision at sea."

"I thought you said that happened when the Ark was still afloat?"

"Not far short of forty years ago. But I found a couple of newspaper cuttings in the back of the booklet and one of 'em is a report on the inquest of a member of the crew who was killed in the collision."

Cain rolled a cigarette; he smoked ten to fifteen a day and none at night because his wife objected to the habit, on the grounds of tidiness, not health.

"There was an odd feature about his death. His body was fished out of the sea ten days after the collision and it was starkers, so it seems pretty certain he was naked when he fell.

58

But he had to be out on deck to fall overboard and who's
going to stand around swinging his jewellery in the breeze if
the temperature's cold enough to freeze 'em?"

"Didn't the coroner have something to say about that?"

"Claimed it didn't have any bearing on the cause of Orr's
death."

"Sensible man."

"If one's looking for something out of place . . ."

"One doesn't go back to the Middle Ages. And anyway I'm
not looking. Get out to Upington and find out if there's been
bad blood with neighbours or kids are causing the trouble."
He lit the cigarette and the first inch went up in flames because
it had been badly packed. He swore.

Keen returned to his car, settled behind the wheel, and stared
along the road. It had been a wasted journey – the husband
was out at work and the wife seemed to be simple-minded.
Upington, once a large village, now a small town with all the
character of a concrete pillbox, was the kind of place that even
if one approached with a smile, one left with set lips. He
should return to Clunford and seek out a woman who was
required to make a witness statement but was trying to avoid
doing so. But Richly Cross was only five miles further north
and there was a chance that Mrs Ellis would be at home . . .

Sibton Avenue was misnamed. To anyone with even a touch
or romance in his imagination, "Avenue" suggested a tree-
lined road and attractive houses with large gardens; reality
was a long line of small, ugly terrace houses which abutted
directly onto pavements.

He parked five houses down from No. 24, walked back and
knocked. The door was opened by a woman of roughly his
age, whose most immediately noticeable feature was her large
brown eyes. He introduced himself. "I rang you yesterday and
you told me there was some difficulty in meeting, so as I was in
the neighbourhood, I thought I'd see if you were at home."

"You'd better come in."

The hall was small and made even smaller by the steep stairs which led directly out of it; the front room was sparsely furnished.

"We've only recently moved in and there's not been time to get everything arranged," she said, as if he had queried the lack of carpet, the worn covers of the two armchairs, the pile of books to the right of the blocked-up fireplace.

"It took us more than a year to get sorted out," he said, trying to forge a warmer atmosphere than there seemed to be. It was a lie. Anne, efficient Anne, had had everything in its place in no time at all.

"We had to move unexpectedly. My husband died." She spoke with defensive abruptness.

"I'm sorry to hear that."

"It happens . . . Do you want some tea or coffee?"

"Please don't bother."

She sat.

Slightly nonplussed by her manner, he settled on the second armchair; a spring twanged. "You'll have been in touch with the hospital, of course."

"No."

He had not expected to have to tell her the news and felt brief resentment that this should be so. "I'm afraid your uncle died yesterday in hospital," he said, more abruptly than he might have done.

"Oh!" She was silent for a few seconds. She looked at him and then away. "I suppose now you're wondering why I'm not overcome by grief?"

"It's none of my business how the news affects you."

"Good." She checked the time. "I'll have to fetch Sandra before long. She hates the new school because she's the newcomer and the others are being beastly to her, but I can't take her away and try another."

"Children can be cruel . . . As I mentioned over the phone,

60

because we need to identify your uncle's next of kin, we had to break into his house and that's where we found your Christmas card—"

She interrupted him. "I had half a dozen left over from last Christmas." She paused, then said bitterly: "God knows why I sent him one with this address. Blood must be thicker than bile."

He began to wonder if she was as mentally disturbed as the woman he'd spoken to before coming there.

She might have read his mind. "I suppose you're wondering just how callous I am?"

"Mrs Ellis, all I want to do is explain . . ."

"After I have. And I've no real idea why I'm going to, but I suppose I'm being a slave to the convention that one's always shocked by the news of a relative's death – and it's so very obvious that I'm not . . . Since you're a detective, maybe you'll understand more readily than most. When I was thirteen, he started touching me up. When I told my mother that, she accused me of making it all up, because she was fond of her brother, but then, when she finally had to believe me, she said she was sure he'd been tight and it would never happen again and I mustn't tell my father because if I did there'd be a terrible family row. Not long afterwards, my uncle called at our house when both my parents were out and he became so excited he tried to rape me. When my father heard this and that I'd told my mother about the previous trouble, he was so furious that he said horrible things to her. Two days later she had a serious stroke and was dead within six months. Because of my age, I thought her death was all my fault . . . Perhaps now you'll understand why I wasn't upset to hear about the accident, haven't been in touch with the hospital, and although you've told me he's dead, I'm not shedding tears. But what you won't be able to understand, any more than I can, is why I sent him my new address."

61

He spoke quietly. "There's something about blood relationships that defies all logic."

She fidgeted with a button on her dress. She stood. "I need a drink. Would you like one?"

"If you're in a rush . . ."

"I'm not. I told you that as an insurance."

"Then I'd like a drink."

"There's only a limited choice – gin, whisky, or sherry."

He asked for a gin and tonic. He watched her leave the room and noted that her figure was neat and she dressed to its advantage.

She returned, handed him a glass. "I hope there's enough gin in it, but if there isn't, say so and I'll add more. I always left the drinks to Ralph and since he died I've had little practice in getting things right." She sat.

He drank. "It's exactly right."

"I wonder! Ralph said my first Yorkshire pudding was perfect, but we both knew it was a gooey failure . . . I'm talking far too much about things that can't interest you. I must be making you very embarrassed as well as bored. There's nothing worse than other people's troubled life histories."

"Neither embarrassed, nor bored. You've managed to explain things."

"Hopefully, that I'm not the kind of person you imagined me to be?"

"I never make hasty judgements."

For the first time, she smiled briefly. "Skirting the truth with evasion?"

That smile had chased away the lines of sad bitterness; she was more attractive than he had first judged. Her features were those of the outdoor woman, not the catwalk beauty. "Shall I now shame the devil and tell you the truth? Your attitude did surprise me. But surprise is a very common occurrence in my job. Lots of people don't carry on their lives as one would expect."

The phone rang. She put her glass down. "Will you excuse me?" She stood, left the room. When she returned, she said, as she settled: "The mother of one of the other girls wanted to know if Sandra could have lunch with her daughter. I said, of course. Hopefully, it means Sandra is beginning to make friends. She'll be a lot happier and that will help her get over what's happened to us." She stared into the past.

He waited for a while, then said: "I don't want to bother you any longer than I need, but I do have to ask a few questions."

"There's no rush. And to be frank, it's nice to have someone to talk to . . . Your glass looks empty. Can I refill it?"

"Thanks, but you'd better not. One of the lads on car patrol today has a natural gift for stopping and breathalysing anyone who's even fractionally over the limit . . . I gather Mr Noyes and his wife moved to Kingsholte a few years back. Was that when he retired?"

"As far as I know, but as you'll have gathered, I had as little as possible to do with him."

"What was his job?"

"He was a ship's steward."

"What?"

"Is that so surprising?"

"In a way, yes, it is. Have you any idea of the names of the ships he served on?"

"None whatsoever."

"Or the company he worked for?"

"I'm sorry."

"Can you suggest any way of finding out?"

Much as Miss Logan had questioned him the previous day, she said: "There's something funny about his death, isn't there?"

"Why d'you ask?"

"Because I'm quite certain you normally wouldn't be interested in what job the victim of a road accident had before he retired several years before."

He hesitated. "There is a slight possibility it wasn't a straightforward hit-and-run," he finally said.

"Why?"

"The car was right over on the wrong side of the road and he must have been in full view for at least a few hundred yards, yet there were no signs the driver tried to swerve back on to his own side, or to brake."

"He was drunk?"

"That would be unusual at a quarter past nine in the morning."

"You're saying it was deliberate?"

"I'm trying to find out if it could have been."

"Just because the car was on the wrong side of the road and the driver didn't brake?"

"And because there was a large sum of cash in the house."

"That is surprising! How much?"

"A hundred and sixty-two thousand pounds."

"Good grief! Where on earth did he manage to get that sort of money? Robbing a bank?"

"Rather unlikely. We wondered if he could have been a miser and that was his life's savings."

"From the little I heard, he was a spender rather than a saver, and mostly his spending wouldn't have recommended him to the local vicar."

"Mrs Ellis—"

"Laura."

"Laura. Do you think he could have been mixed up in drug trafficking?"

"To be honest, it wouldn't exactly surprise me."

"But you've no idea whether he actually was?"

"None. And if I'd ever suspected that, I'd have told the authorities," she said, with sudden sharpness. "I don't like informing, but drugs frighten me because of children."

"So you can't suggest where that money might have come from?"

"I'm sorry to keep saying the same thing, but I knew so little about him. When Meg was alive I would have liked to have seen something of her because she was a kindly person – God knows why she ever married him – but I knew that if he were in the house, he'd be watching me with eyes that were wondering what I'd do if he reached up under my skirt."

Did a man's eyes always disclose his baser thoughts? He hoped not. "Thanks for being so helpful."

"I rather get the impression that I've been anything but."

He smiled. "I've only one more question. Would you know who is Mr Noyes's heir?"

"I've no idea."

"And you are his nearest relative?"

"He and Meg had no children and she was an only child."

"Can you give me the names of any of his friends?"

"That's three questions!"

"I always was hopeless at maths. If you could name someone, I might be able to find out what shipping company he was with."

"Once again, I'm useless. I just can't help you. Off the cuff, I'd say he probably didn't have any friends, but that's being bitchy."

"Understandably. Then I'll leave you in peace." He stood. "If there's anything more you might want to ask, call back."

"I'll do just that."

She accompanied him to the front door and smiled as she said goodbye. He walked along to his car, drove off. When he reached the countryside and the road was relatively free of traffic, he allowed his thoughts to turn to Laura Ellis. For years and in the face of logic, she had blamed herself for her mother's death; her husband had died recently, leaving her to bring up their daughter in what obviously were straitened circumstances. Could the mental self-chastisement have merged with the mental pain to provide a motive for revenge? She might have had knowledge of the money hidden in the house and that she was his heir, or have gambled that he'd die intestate. What colour car did she drive? He found himself wishing his job didn't call on him to be ready to search for dark, hidden motives.

Eight

C ain's tone was surly. "If you'd walked you couldn't have taken any longer."

"You don't know how slowly I can walk," Keen replied, as he stood in front of the desk.

"Did you manage to reach Akers Road before you became completely immobile?"

"The husband was out and the wife's missing some of her marbles so there was precious little joy. When I asked her what was nicked this time, she couldn't tell me. The husband's a long-distance lorry driver and she thinks he'll be back tomorrow, or is she mixing it up with the previous week? I'll try again."

"Forget it. I'll send someone who can run." Cain relit a cigarette which had gone out.

"Incidentally, since Richly Cross was only a few minutes away, I took the opportunity to call in and have a word with Mrs Ellis."

"You set your own itinerary these days?"

"Surely we needed to know if she can help us?"

Cain grunted reluctant agreement.

Keen decided not to repeat some of what she had told him because Cain had a crude sense of humour and would have seen Noyes's behaviour as reason for sniggering. "She doesn't know who's the heir and can't name any friends; but did say that he'd been a ship's steward."

"Like I said at the beginning, drugs. Half the crew of any ship is running something."

"Noyes retired some years ago."

"So when he was at sea he had an eye to the future and built up a stock which he's been selling off ever since. Where did he sail to?"

"She doesn't know what company he worked for. But I'll give you ten to one it was the Aylton Shipping Company."

"Where did their ships go to?"

"I've no idea."

"Then I'll tell you. The land of coke. Bolivia."

"Wouldn't they have found docking rather difficult?"

"How's that?"

Keen remained silent. Cain's sense of humour did not extend to himself.

"Like as not there's something about the house that'll tell us more." He spoke more aggressively. "But I'll guarantee you never thought to find out."

"We searched the hall and then went up to the bedroom; when we found the money, nothing else mattered."

"With your generation, nothing does matter. Search the house again and this time try to do a proper job. The back door key's been got from the hospital and it's down in Property."

"You want me to go there now?"

"This time next year will be stretching things a bit too much even for the likes of you."

"I'll get moving."

"That'll be a bloody change."

Keen drove past the bungalow – he caught a glimpse of an arched behind in a blue dress; Miss Logan dragging out a weed which had dared to appear overnight? – rounded the corner, turned into the short drive of Noyes's house. After climbing out of the car, he went forward to the side of the detached garage and peered through the window. Inside was a BMW saloon; in the 500 range, he judged. Whatever the source of the money, it had been a generous one.

He unlocked the kitchen door and entered. He checked the refrigerator/deep freeze and found both compartments to be three-quarters full. The food in the deep freeze would probably keep until the question of who now owned the house was established, but that in the refrigerator would not. It would have to be cleared and – the appropriate forms filled in – the food thrown away. If so much as one pot of yoghurt was eaten, there would be cause for a charge of theft. The law really could be, ". . . a ass, a idiot."

He went upstairs and searched the three bedrooms, uncovered nothing fresh. However, in the desk in the sitting room he struck gold. Amongst the jumble of more brochures for luxury cruises – again, all from one company – was an address book and four Discharge Books.

He examined the address book and was disappointed by the paucity of entries. It seemed Noyes had few friends with whom he had kept in touch. Judging by the kind of man he was, perhaps that was hardly surprising. He picked up one of the Discharge Books, not knowing what it was, learned it was an official record of the ships on which the holder had served and his conduct during each voyage. In the second book, it was recorded that Noyes had sailed on SS *Slecome Bay* between June 1961 and October 1963.

Drew rubbed his chin with forefinger and thumb. "It certainly would call for an unusual coincidence if there were no connection."

Cain and Keen were seated on the other side of the desk; Cain's expression was disgruntled.

"On the other hand, I suppose one could say that coincidences never stop being unusual . . . What do we know about the shipping company? Does it even still exist?"

They were silent.

69

"It might be an idea to find out as much about it as we can," he said with mild sarcasm. "And specifically, does it trade with ports noted for drugs?"

"We'll check on that right away," Cain said, trying to bring back an air of efficiency.

Keen said: "Sir, I think . . ."

"I can probably guess what you think. But until we have reason to believe otherwise, we'll take the obvious line and assume the source of the money is drugs."

Keen would have liked to argue the wisdom of that, but Drew was not a man to have his decisions challenged.

"It seems odd Mrs Ellis can't offer the name of a single friend, even allowing for the fact that clearly she was not very fond of her uncle."

"Once Mrs Noyes had died, there was hardly any contact."

"Then why did she send the card with her new address?"

"I don't suppose she could give you a solid answer. Probably it was an irrational act. She's been badly hit by her husband's death and at such time a relative can provide the comforting illusion of someone to turn to, even when one really knows that to ask for any kind of help would be a complete waste of time."

"Move over, Dr Freud," Cain said.

Drew was annoyed by the puerile remark, but made no comment. "Did you learn why there was such antagonism on her part?"

"No, sir."

"Someone said that the greatest riddle facing mankind is man . . . You say there are only very few names in the address book. Get onto them. With a bit of luck, one will prove to be an old shipmate. A ship must be a very enclosed society where it's difficult to do anything without other people knowing about it . . . Where are we with the car?"

Cain answered him. "The stolen lists of the past seven days have been checked. We would strike a real busy time! One hundred and twenty-six possibles. But there is one lead that could save a lot of effort. A burned-out grey Audi estate, stolen in Newcastle on Saturday, found this morning in a clearing in a wood, five miles north of Birmingham; it definitely wasn't there Sunday night."

"Have you asked for further details?"

"Yes, but they aren't through yet. I specifically noted a broken nearside headlamp. If the Audi's got one, we can have a comparison test made with the glass fragments found on the road."

Drew leaned back in his chair. "Nicked the Audi up north, came south, lined up Noyes and ran him down; back up Birmingham way, torched the Audi, transferred into a clean car and a quiet journey home . . . Possible. But we could be constructing a murder when all that happened is Joe Soaks was driving even more carelessly than usual." He was silent for several seconds. "Let's turn up some answers." He nodded to show the meeting was at an end.

In the corridor, before he turned into his own room, Cain said: "Find out about the company and check through all the names in the address book. But don't spend so long over that that all your other cases go slack."

Covering himself on both sides, Keen thought. Perhaps one had to learn to do that before one could safely wear sergeant's stripes. He continued on into the CID general room.

Clayton, seated by the window, said: "Where's Archbold?" When he retired, he was moving to Shetland. Which, according to Parr, showed that when young, he'd been dropped on his head.

"It was on one of the desks the last time I saw it," Keen replied, as he stood by the table and reached for the first volume of the London telephone directory.

"It's not on anybody's desk now. Nothing ever gets put back."

Archbold's Criminal Pleading, Evidence and Practice should have been in the bookcase in the detective sergeant's room; it very seldom was. Once seated at his desk, Keen riffled through the pages of the directory and found an entry for Aylton Shipping Company, Ltd – it still existed. He dialled the first of the numbers listed and suffered the usual irritation of music-while-you-wait before he spoke to a woman in the general office. His questions intrigued her, but she readily answered them without querying his reason for asking them. The company had been founded soon after the end of World War Two and a Liberty ship had been purchased from the British government. The company had expanded slowly but skilfully and now the fleet numbered eight ships with one more contracted for. This ninth vessel would be eighteen thousand tons.

It was clear he was meant to be impressed and he tried to give the impression that he was even though the ship sounded rather like a Dinky toy when two- and three-hundred-thousand-ton tankers were regularly running aground. "I'm interested in the *Slecome Bay*, which was at sea in the early sixties."

"That's long before I joined the company."

He hastily assured her he never doubted that. "I'm just hoping you'll be able to tell me something about it."

"I can't, but maybe Mr Benson will be able to. He's been with the company for a long time. I'll put you through."

He presumed Benson enjoyed memories of hauling on the clew lines or whatever it was one hauled on when in the Roaring Forties.

"I gather you're asking about the *Slecome Bay*?" Benson's voice made him think of a small man with a dusty, bald head. "All I can tell you about her is that some years ago she was sold to a South Korean firm for scrap. I always think how sad it is for a ship that has sailed the seven seas to end so ignominiously."

It seemed the dusty, bald head housed a sense of romance. "In 1963, she was in collision with a ship called *Atoka*."

"Of course! And if my memory now begins to serve me, the

collision became a textbook example of the dangers of not plotting the radar bearings of an oncoming vessel."

"In a roundabout way, it's because of that collision I'm interested in it."

"I see," Benson said, plainly not doing so.

"Back in those days, where would it have been sailing to?"

"Please forgive me saying this, but a ship is always 'she'."

"Apologies all round. Where would she have sailed to?"

"There can be no immediate answer to your question, Mr Keen. You see, in one sense we have always been a tramping company since no ship has a fixed itinerary and even at the start of a voyage it may not be certain what are all the ports to which she will be sailing. But please understand that in another sense, our ships most certainly are not tramps. They are maintained to the highest standards and the accommodation will bear comparison with any vessel afloat."

"Are you saying that the *Slecome Bay* could have sailed to any port in the world?"

"Indeed. Although remembering that the Cold War was in progress, there would be some ports it was most unlikely she visited."

"Are there records you can check to find out exactly where she did go in sixty-one, two, and three?"

"I suppose so. Despite the space they occupy, the rough logbooks of all the ships the company has ever owned are kept in store. But it would present a great deal of work."

"It could help us a great deal."

"Then I will see what can be done."

"That's really kind of you. One final question. Does a Mr Cedric Searle have any connection with the company?"

There was a dry chuckle. "I am tempted to answer, just a little! Mr Searle is our chairman and managing director; his wife is a majority shareholder."

Bingo again!

*   *   *

On his return to home and loneliness, he poured himself a very solid gin and tonic. He sat in front of the television and channel-hopped, found nothing he wanted to watch. He drained his glass, thought to hell with it, went through to the hall, picked up the telephone receiver and dialled.

"Richly Cross four seven one six," Laura said.

"It's Mike."

"Who?"

"Mike Keen, local CID. I had a word with you this morning."

"Oh, dear, I am slow, aren't I? . . . Have I inadvertently damaged the male ego?"

"It's so battered that another little dent won't show."

"I must say, it didn't strike me as at all damaged."

"I was brought up to show a brave face even when on the rack."

"But sometimes it's not so easy to follow instructions, is it?"

Light, meaningless repartee had suddenly brought painful memories rushing in. "I'm very sorry."

"For what?"

"Talking nonsense."

"You wouldn't think of apologising if you knew what fun it is to listen to nonsense when the world's mostly so very serious."

"Then perhaps . . ."

"What?"

"You'd like to come out for a drink and listen to some more?"

"When?"

"They say there's no time like the present."

"No can do."

The brush off? "Perhaps some other time, then?"

"It's not that I don't want to, but I can't leave Sandra on her own. But is there anything to stop you coming here for the drink and to talk nonsense?"

74

No brush off. "Not if I'm invited."

"Do you want the invitation engraved or, in this egalitarian age, will printed do?"

"I'll be with you in twenty minutes if the traffic's normal, fifteen if it's light."

"Take care."

She wore some make-up, a more colourful dress, and she greeted him with a smile. He handed her a bottle of gin.

"There was no need for this."

"It was my invitation."

"Then thank you very much. Now, come on through and meet Sandra."

Sandra, round face topped by curly black hair, was watching television.

"This is Mr Keen," Laura said, as she put the gin down on a tray on which were two bottles, two glasses, and a small bowlful of crisps.

Sandra, who was sitting on one of the chairs, looked briefly at Keen, then back at the screen.

"A good evening would sound nice."

She pressed her lips tightly together.

"Come on, poppet, lighten up."

Continuing silence.

"Please, don't be awkward." Laura looked at Keen, asking for sympathetic understanding.

He smiled to suggest he understood perfectly. In truth, he probably did. Sandra was spoiled.

"It's time for bed," Laura said.

"No, it isn't," Sandra replied.

"You know it is."

"I want to watch this programme."

"You promised me you'd go straight up without any fuss after you'd met Mr Keen. And you haven't even said hullo to him!"

"I want to watch the programme."

Keen listened as Laura asked, pleaded, even threatened in a tone that wouldn't have cowed a frightened rabbit. Finally, with a sulky refusal to say goodnight to him, Sandra allowed herself to be led out of the room after Laura had told him to help himself a drink.

He poured out a gin and tonic, sat. If Judy had behaved like that, Anne would have . . . He drank. A great time to think of Anne!

Laura said, as she stepped into the room several minutes later: "I'm sorry Sandra was being difficult."

"Forget it."

"She was very tired and . . ." She became silent.

"And behaving like every other kid does some time or another. Let me get you a drink."

She sat in the second armchair.

"What's yours?"

"A G and T, please." She watched him pour the drink. "She's been through so much."

"You both have," he said as he handed her the glass.

"When she behaves like that, she's probably trying to get her own back on life."

"Why not, if it helps?"

"You're very understanding. You must have children of your own?"

"A daughter who can make Sandra's effort seem tame." But only very briefly, because Anne would soon make certain she changed her manners.

"You're a married man, then?"

"That rather depends on definitions. My wife decided my lifestyle and hers weren't compatible and we've separated. It happens a lot in the force."

"I suppose work keeps you away from home too often?"

"That's part of the problem."

"Life's difficult for so many people, isn't it?"

"And once again, my talking nonsense has ended badly."

"It's my fault for being curious." She fiddled with her glass, then drank quickly. "I suffer from the annoying complaint of wanting to know the truth about people; to understand the face behind the mask."

"I look better with my mask on."

She smiled. "I suspect we all do and that's why we wear them."

At a quarter past nine, he said, "I'd better start moving."

"I could offer you a cold supper if you don't have to rush."

"My sergeant would assure you that I'm incapable of rushing."

"Then I'll go through to the kitchen and prepare things."

As she stood, he said: "Is the Volvo parked outside yours?"

"That's a neighbour's – he's the kind of man who delights in parking in front of someone else's house. Rumour has it he draws Social Security for all his cousins and nephews as well as himself in order to keep both of his expensive cars on the road. We did have a Volvo, but I had to sell it after Ralph's death and now I drive around in a clapped-out Fiesta."

"The red one half a dozen cars along?"

"It's green." She crossed to the door, came to a halt and swung round. "Why are you asking about my car?"

"I've always been interested in Volvos and if it had been yours, I'd have asked what you thought about it."

"Yet when you heard I had a Fiesta, you wanted to know what colour it was."

He could have talked about passing a Fiesta that seemed to be parked too far out from the pavement for safety, but decided to accept that his questioning had been less than subtle and she was sharper than he had allowed. "If your car had been grey, that fact might have been significant."

"How?"

"The car which knocked your uncle down was grey."

She stared at him. "And you thought I might have been driving the car that killed him?"

"I was quite sure you weren't. But in my job, everything has to be double-checked."

"Why on earth could I possibly want to kill him?"

"Because of what happened in the past."

"You can't understand that I do my best to forget rather than remember by nursing hatred? So the reason for this visit is underhand official and not, as you've tried to make me believe, social." Her tone was bitter.

"It was my job to check what colour your car is. So I tried to work out how to do that without upsetting you. Questioning you directly was out because you'd be bound to be distressed. I decided to do it casually, but having a tongue that never kissed the Blarney Stone, I've made a BU of things. But if you think that that's why I'm here now, you're a hundred and one per cent mistaken. If my only motive had been to learn about the car, I'd have come during the day, when I was working. I'm here now because I wanted to see you again."

"Is that the truth?"

"Cut my throat if every word isn't a pearl of veracity."

"I wonder if I have a knife sharp enough." She turned back and left.

He arrived home to find the phone ringing.

"I've been trying to get you for the last two hours," Anne said. "I suppose you've been in a boozer, telling the lads you wife doesn't understand you."

"I've been out on a job."

"I'll bet!"

"You sound as if something's wrong?"

"Judy's in hospital."

"My God! What's wrong?"

"They think it's a viral infection. She's to have more tests tomorrow."

"How ill is she?"

"Ill enough. But it's not dangerous yet and they hope they've acted in time."

"Tell them . . ." He stopped. Anne would do whatever was necessary. She guarded Judy with all the ferocity of a vixen protecting her cubs. "I'll try and get time off tomorrow to see her."

"There's no need. The hospital allows mothers to be with children so I've arranged to cut work and be with her most of the day."

"It doesn't occur to you that I might want to see her?"

"Frankly, I'm certain you'd rather continue boozing with the lads. I'll let you know what the results of the tests are." She cut the connection.

He wondered if she'd have been less bitchy had he been at home when she first called.

Nine

Wednesday brought clear skies, a soft, warm wind, and the hint of summer. Drew was not in tune with the weather; he was at his most abrupt. "Yes?" He looked back at the papers he was putting into a briefcase.

Keen said: "I had a word with an old boy in the Aylton Shipping Company, sir, and learned something interesting. Cedric Searle is chairman of the company and his wife's a major shareholder."

Drew put the last paper into the briefcase, closed it, secured the first of the holding straps. "So?"

"The second newspaper cutting in the collision report was the announcement of Searle's wedding."

Drew secured the second strap. "Are you certain it's the same Cedric Searle?"

"Not at the moment. But all I have to do is ask him."

"And then what?"

"Assuming he is the same man, find out how he fits into the picture."

"In other words, if he played any part in the murder of Noyes, always assuming he was murdered?"

"Yes."

"Do you have any idea who this Cedric Searle might be?"

"I've said all I know about him."

"You're not a reader of the gossip columns? 'The' Cedric Searle was, as he proudly tells anyone and everyone, born on the bottom rung of life and has spent his life clawing his way up to the top one. He's the archetypal rags-to-riches and every time some spotty nerd makes a billion or two out of computing, he's referred to as a second Searle. He's married to a woman who's on friendly terms with minor royalty and he's such a loyal supporter of the government he's been appointed an adviser to them on maritime matters; reputedly, he's to be ennobled, presumably to prove the age of equality has arrived for those who have no need of it. But of far more relevance to us is the fact that he was chairman of the local Police Authority; and that when Bill Francis was forced to resign on grounds that shouldn't have been held to be sufficient for anything but a minor reprimand, rumour said there was some personal reason for Searle's pursuing the matter so fiercely. Perhaps Bill was screwing his wife. I hope so. Bill was, and is, a good friend and nothing would give me greater pleasure than to arrest Searle on a serious charge. But because of all the clout he carries, I've no intention of disturbing his wealthy peace, even by asking him the time of day, until we have far greater reason than a newspaper cutting from the past."

"But—"

"That appears to have become a favourite word of yours."

Keen left.

He phoned the names that had been written down in the address book from Noyes's desk. Not until the eighth call did he receive the answer he'd been hoping for.

"Yeah, I was at sea with him."

"On the *Slecome Bay*?"

"That's right. And we was together on another ship. Don't remember her name right now, but I'll think of it."

"I'm sorry to have to tell you that Mr Noyes had an accident from which he unfortunately died."

"Is that so? The poor old sod!"

"And it's because of the accident that we're interested in his time at sea. If someone comes along to your house, will you be willing to tell him what you can?"

"Can't see why not. But I don't get what this is all about."

"It'll be explained to you." Keen rang off. He telephoned the Thames Valley police and asked the liaison officer at HQ to arrange for Mr Thomas Foster, Kenshall Cottage, Upper Lipton, to be interviewed.

When the request for a witness to be questioned was received from another force, there was never any doubt what priority that request would be accorded – the lowest. It was Saturday before PC Sendall, seconded to CID, parked in front of Kenshall Cottage, a modern, brick-built bungalow which had a weathervane that featured a square-rigger.

Mrs Foster, elderly and no longer bothering to dress with care, said that Dad was out at the back and she'd get him. Sendall waited with growing impatience in the sitting room.

Foster finally entered. "Been planting peas. According to the weather bloke on the telly, it's going to rain and I want 'em in before it does. There's nothing like some rain to get seeds sprouting, is there?"

As far as Sendall was concerned, peas came from supermarkets. However, despite his impatience, he managed to say, in the cause of public relations: "Good of you to have a word with me, Mr Foster."

"Didn't get no option. Someone rang and said as you'd be coming here." As he slumped down on the nearest chair, Foster's expression was disgruntled.

Still yards of peas to be sown before the next rain? "You know Mr Noyes has unfortunately died in an accident?"

"Poor old sod. And I remember now. She was the *Skemarrow Bay*."

"How's that?"

"You know."

"I don't," Sendall replied, his impatience finally becoming obvious.

"The other ship we was both on. There was trouble with the engines and we was in Durban for several weeks. Me and Reg . . ." He was silent for several seconds, then said: "The randiest bastard I ever sailed with. I'm telling you, he couldn't look at any woman, didn't matter what she was like, without wondering what his chances were. I said to him, 'Carry on like this, mate, and you'll wear yourself out if a husband doesn't come along first and stick a knife into you.' But it never happened. Unless that's what did kill him?"

"He was involved in a car accident."

"I remember now. That's what the bloke said as happened."

"Did you sail with him to South or Central America?"

"Ended up in Murmansk once. Bloody unfriendly natives. But you know something – Reg found a woman even there!"

"Whereabouts in America did you go?"

"Everywhere. Never knew where you might be sailing to next."

"Did you often go to Central America?"

"He near got knifed in Veracruz. The woman's bloke came back unexpected and Reg had to leg it with nothing but an old towel to wrap around himself. We had a good laugh at him when he scuttled aboard, I can tell you."

The questions continued; the answers added up to two facts – the ships had sailed the seven seas and Reg had found a woman in every port.

"And he weren't even good-looking," Foster said resentfully.

"But he obviously had something!"

"I'll tell you what he had. No taste and an old woman what didn't ask what he'd been doing. Not like my old woman. Every time I came home it was, what did you do, why didn't you write more often, was you too busy with some rotten little tart to bother with your wife? I'll tell you, there's some is lucky and some that ain't."

Sendall steered the conversation to smuggling.

"I kept me hands clean; weren't worth the risk. The company had rules – get caught and you was out on your ear."

"But I expect there were those who didn't worry about the rules?"

"There's always a few daft sods."

"So what did they mostly smuggle?"

"Booze, fags, porno from Rotterdam, only there wasn't much profit in that. Too much of it around already."

"Did anyone try drugs?"

"Only if he were raving. There was a greaser called . . . What was his name? I'll forget me own next . . . Sam, that's it. It was on me first trip with 'em after I left the company what wanted two days' work for one day's pay. Sam bought several kilos of hash in Casablanca and hid it in between the pipes inside the funnel. Spent the rest of the trip saying he was going to buy a house with the money he'd make. Only the customs was waiting for him in Hull and it didn't take 'em no time to find the stuff. People said he was shopped by the bloke what sold it to him – smart bastard ended up with the reward money as well as what he'd got paid for the hash. Put people off, that did, when Sam got sent down for three years."

"You don't think it's possible Noyes was handling drugs and keeping dead quiet about it?"

"You don't keep nothing quiet aboard. Anyways, that wasn't his style. Didn't like taking risks except where women was concerned."

"You were with him on the *Slecome Bay* when it was in collision?"

"There was me, him and . . . What was his name? Alf? Roger? . . . I can't recollect. Anyways, we shared a cabin."

"So if, in fact, he had been smuggling, you'd almost certainly have known about it?"

"If you're talking about that trip, all he was concerned with was one of the passengers." Foster laughed coarsely. "She was married, but she wore skirts what had a man checking his shoe laces. And that had the Second sniffing around her as if he was suffering shortage of air. He didn't know Reg was already keeping her crow's nest warm." He sniggered. "The Second had the gold stripes, but Reg had something what weighed more . . . Had a real laugh one night, he did. Come to think of it, can't have been more'n a couple of days before the collision. He always turned off the alleyway lights when he was knocking her so as none of the other passengers would see him using her cabin and this night someone crashed into him in the dark just as he was leaving. It was Terry and since Terry wasn't a passenger steward, being in the accommodation would've had him sacked. He took off like he was tied to a rocket."

"Who was Terry?"

"Can't remember his other name."

"And he was shagging another woman passenger?" Sendall asked with prurient interest.

"Not him. He liked his meat boiled, not grilled."

Sendall checked his notebook in which he'd noted the questions he'd been asked to make. "Can you remember any of the other passengers on the trip?"

"Like I just said, I wasn't a passenger steward so all I saw was them lolling about on deck or in the saloon. But that's not to forget Reg's bit what sometimes stood by the rails on the sun deck and didn't mind who was below and looking up to admire the view."

"So you wouldn't know if one of the passengers was called Cedric Searle."

"That's where you're wrong, mate! Chris – that's the name of the bloke I couldn't remember. Smart dresser was Chris."

"What about him?"

"Chris told me, over a can of beer, that one of the passengers called Searle knew which side his bread was buttered on because he was engaged to the daughter of the bloke what founded the company. Said that if the bloke ever took over, things would get tough because he looked a real hard case. But I made several voyages after Searle became chairman and nothing much changed. In that company, things was always run on a tight hawser – officers on the bridge in reefers, stewards in white jackets. And the Old Man on the *Slecome* would've had everyone saluting if he hadn't known the salute would've been two fingers. Miserable old bastard, he was."

Sendall closed the notebook. "Thanks for your time."

"It's all I've got plenty of these days."

Keen read the faxed report, carried it through to Cain. "Just come in, Sarge."

"It's taken 'em long enough."

"It always takes for ever."

"Any request made to us gets dealt with very promptly."

"And two hundred and fifty-one angels can stand on the head of a pin."

"You're getting too bloody smart for your own good!" Cain slowly read through the report. He put it down on the desk, sat back in the chair. "Doesn't take us any further."

"You don't reckon it cuts out drug running?"

"Because Foster says there wasn't any? He would say that, wouldn't he?"

"I suppose so. Still, it does tell us 'the' Cedric Searle was aboard the *Slecome Bay* when she collided with the *Atoka* and his marriage to Berenice Ambrose was important as far as Noyes was concerned."

"Does it?"

"The marriage announcement was in the deed box."

"People keep newspaper cuttings just because they were alive and around at the time. My mother had a scrapbook filled with cuttings about the Royal Family and Lloyd George. Doesn't mean she had tea with 'em. You seem determined to make a mountain out of a bloody molehill."

"There is a hundred and sixty-two thousand, seven hundred

87

and fifty quid in cash to account for, not forgetting a BMW in the garage and a house worth several hundred thousand."

Cain began to roll a cigarette.

"You read about Noyes bumping into someone in the passenger accommodation and thinking it was an officer, but finding it was Terry?"

"Well?"

"It must have been Terry Orr."

Cain lit the edge of the paper, stuck it down. "You don't think there might just have been two blokes aboard called Terry?" He lit a match. Almost inevitably, the end of the cigarette disappeared in flame as he drew on it.

"Assume it was Orr. What was he doing in the passenger accommodation when he wasn't a passenger steward and he would have been sacked if found there?"

"Since they bumped into each other near the cabin in which was the tart Noyes was shagging, maybe he'd been harvesting his oats first."

"Except there's an indication in the report that Orr's tastes weren't the same as Noyes's. Maybe he was DC."

"And if he was?"

"We'd be close to understanding why he was fished out of the water naked. I reckon we need Foster questioned again and asked if Orr was a homosexual. And if he ever saw Orr wearing a signet ring similar to the one we found in the deed box."

Ten

T he phone rang as Keen opened the front door. He
crossed the hall, picked up the receiver.

"I'm back at Fay's," Anne said. "The hospital likes
mothers to leave by six unless the child is really ill. I think
she's quite a bit better, but she's not so certain. Rather likes
the attention."

"Thank goodness for that. I know you said not to, but I
nipped in to see her this morning."

"She told me when I got back from some shopping. She
showed me the book you bought her."

"I thought it would be more appreciated than the traditional bunch of grapes."

"I had to read her several pages because her eyes were so
tired."

"Have you mentioned that to someone?"

"It was me reading that she wanted. She reckoned that if she
said her eyes were tired, I wouldn't tell her to do the reading
because it was good for her."

"And being the smart mum you are, you didn't let on you'd
rumbled her . . . So how are you?"

"Mentally exhausted."

"But you can begin to relax now?"

"How would you suggest I go about doing that? Down at
the pub?"

He hid his resentment at that unnecessary remark. "How
are things at Malcolm House?"

"Fay's being wonderful and fussing around me as if I were the patient."

"I expect she's glad to have something definite to do."

"Can't resist the sly dig, can you?"

"I didn't mean it that way," he protested. "Would you like me to go with you to the hospital tomorrow as it's Sunday and I'm not duty officer?"

"I'm quite capable of driving myself."

"It would be company for you."

"If Judy continues to improve and I needn't spend all day with her, Ifor's taking Fay and me out to lunch to some special restaurant that's just started up."

"Does that prevent us going together to the hospital?"

"I'd prefer arrangements to stay as they are."

"Why?"

"If you don't know, there's small point in my trying to explain."

"You're very fond of saying that. I suppose it's because it means you don't have to try to find an explanation."

"Good night, Mike."

"Would you just tell me—" He was talking into a dead phone. He replaced the receiver. The conversation had begun in stilted fashion, as if they were only casual friends, and then had quickly become filled with misunderstanding and resentment. Was this par for the course when a marriage had turned sour? There was irony in the fact that he had been about to drive to Laura's when Anne had phoned.

Laura returned to the sitting room and sat. "How's your glass?"

"Being an optimist, it's still half full."

"Are you an optimist?"

"When I'm not pessimistic."

She picked up her glass and drank. "I'm sorry Sandra was . . . a little difficult."

"What child isn't?"

"At her age, it's almost impossible to understand why life's so hard."

"Not any easier, surely, when one's older?"

"But one can make oneself accept it and not keep saying, if only. Two of the most cruel, bloody useless words in the language. Do you object to women swearing?"

"It gives me the excuse to do the same."

"My father disliked hearing a woman say anything even as strong as 'damn'. I used to say he was a refugee from the Mesozoic era. Mother was far more adaptable, but then women usually are."

"Adaptable or pliable?"

"The kind of male question a sensible female refuses to answer . . . Do you like shepherd's pie?"

"One of my favourites."

"There are times when I simply can't decide whether to believe you, or not."

"You're suggesting I might be a liar?"

"I think you reasoned I wouldn't have asked the question unless I'd prepared shepherd's pie for supper and therefore as a polite guest you'd say how much you liked the dish even if you detested it."

"You're crediting me with a far more cunning nature than I have."

"Am I?"

"Anne always says—" He stopped abruptly.

"Mike, I'm not going to be upset just because you mention your wife. What does she say about you?"

"That I may try to conceal myself, but most of the time she can follow my mind, because after one's lived or worked with someone, one knows their line of thought. I suppose she's right. At work, the detective sergeant is the slow and steady type: present him with an unusual, way-out possibility and you know he'll mentally shiver and do his best not to understand. The detective inspector, on the other hand, may appear to think you're talking nonsense, but you can be certain he's ahead of you and has worked out that you could be right but as far as he's concerned, you're wrong."

"I don't follow that."

"Sorry. I'm thinking aloud about something at work; that's rude on any count."

"It's interesting. I want to know more."

"You've asked for it! We've a case in hand where I've put forward a proposition which means we need to face someone who has a lot of influence in the world. The sergeant sees my idea as impossible, full stop. The detective inspector is no keener to take direct action, but I'm certain that's not because he can't understand all the possibilities, he knows that people with clout are quick to use it so he's holding back because there's not the evidence yet and that could leave him in a very exposed position. His first concern is himself and as he's in command, he'd receive all the flak. One of the advantages of being in the ranks is that the final responsibility is someone else's."

"Does that mean you don't intend to go for promotion?"

"Far from it. Just that I recognise promotion has a downside."

She looked at her watch. "I'll go and dish. Do we eat at table or, as Sandra always wants so that we can watch the television, on our laps?"

"I'm sure you've given me the option as there's a programme you like coming up."

"It'll take you quite a lot longer to understand how my mind works! Will a Spanish red with the meal be all right?"

"My favourite."

She laughed.

"I ought to move," he said. To his disappointment, she didn't argue. He stood. "Let's do the same again?"

"Why not?" she answered.

"I'll bring some Chicken Kiev from M&S."

It was her turn to say: "My favourite."

As they went through to the hall, he thought that when people began to share jokes that must be meaningless to anyone else, their relationship had reached a certain stage . . . The hall light was weak and her face was partially in shadow, adding a touch of mystery to her features. "Shall we make the supper date soon?"

"As soon as you like. And shall we eat earlier so that Sandra can be with us?"

He tried to show enthusiasm for the suggestion. "A good idea."

"She so enjoys behaving like a grown-up does. They all do, don't they?"

"Until they become old enough to want to behave like a child."

"That's either clever or smart-alecky and I'm not certain which."

"Then choose the former."

"You wouldn't mind if she ate with us, would you?"

"Of course not."

"You're rather a dear!"

"Then I claim my reward." He kissed her. She did not respond; nor did she miss his disappointment. "It's very early days for both of us, Mike," she whispered.

Perhaps it was for her, even if she'd been widowed some months before, because her separation had been involuntary; it wasn't for him, because Anne had chosen to leave him.

Sendall parked the police Escort, crossed the pavement, and knocked on the front door, was directed round to the back by Foster's wife. Foster was planting out well-developed plants in a rectangular bed of fine, dark soil in front of the kitchen window.

The police manual said an officer should always seize the chance of showing interest in a witness's hobby. "They look like nice plants."

"Ought to be considering they cost a bloody fortune. Says she must have some colour to look out at." Foster jerked his head in the direction of the window. "I could grow real good tomatoes here, but no, she has to have these things." He might have been planting deadly nightshade.

"The ladies like their flowers . . . I've one or two more questions."

Foster stood up. "You've more questions than a dog has fleas. Well, what is they?"

It seemed that not even the barest hospitality was going to be offered. "You remember telling me about Terry?"

"No."

"You said he was with you on the *Slecome Bay* and one night he and Reg Noyes banged into each other in the passenger accommodation and he was scared because he shouldn't have been there?"

"You mean him!"

No. Horatio Nelson. "What was his surname?"

"Can't remember names these days."

"Try."

"What d'you think I'm doing?"

"It's important."

"Why?"

"I don't know."

"Then how come you can say it's important?"

Sendall mentally threw public relations into the dustbin. "Because that's what I was told. And if you're trying to be difficult, you'll find I can be a sight more so."

"There's no call for that. I ain't trying anything. I just don't recollect his surname. All I can tell you is he was the bloke what got killed in the collision. They fished his body out of the sea later on."

"Was he gay?"

"Bit of a misery, really."

"I mean, was he a homosexual?"

"Course he was."

"So what was he doing in the passenger accommodation?"

"You need telling?"

"Do you know the passenger he visited?"

"Here, are you suggesting I was one of them?"

"All I'm doing is asking if you've any idea which passenger he was friendly with."

"Well, I ain't, so it's no good saying different."

"That's fair enough . . . I've something to show you." He passed across colour photographs of the signet ring, viewed from four different angles. "Have you ever seen this before?"

"Couldn't say."

"Perhaps someone aboard a ship was wearing it?"

"I keep telling you, when you reach my age, things is hazy. That's what I say to her inside, but she still goes on and on at me for forgetting. No thought for others, that's her."

"If you should remember, like one sometimes does when one's not trying, give us a buzz at the station. Here's the number." He brought out from his pocket a small card with the telephone number of divisional HQ on it. "Shall I write my name down so as you don't forget it?"

Foster shrugged his shoulders.

Sendall wrote, passed the card across. He had begun to walk around the corner of the house when a shout stopped him. He turned back.

Foster, once more kneeling, a trowel in one hand, looked up. "I kind of think I saw him with something like that ring."

"Saw who?"

"Terry. That's who you was talking about, ain't it? Always showing it off. And one day Chiefy saw it and asked him if he'd got it out of a Christmas cracker? Sarcastic bastard, Chiefy was. I've seen a bloke near in tears because of what

Chief had said to him. But he never tried anything on me. Knew he'd get as good as he gave."

Sendall wrote down this last information, neither knowing nor caring whether it was of the slightest importance.

"It all fits, Guv'nor," Keen said on Monday morning as he stood in front of the desk.

"Like a size eight shoe fits my size eleven feet," Drew replied shortly.

"We know the cash has a smell."

"We surmise. We don't know."

"The reports of the collision and the inquest, the cutting announcing the marriage, the signet ring, say there has to be a connection. Searle was being blackmailed."

"Over what?"

"His relationship with Orr aboard the *Slecome Bay*."

"According to the report, Foster has no idea who Orr was visiting."

"The ring was given to Orr on the trip on which Searle was a passenger."

"I don't recollect any evidence to suggest it was on that trip that Foster may have seen him wearing it. And is it your suggestion that Searle carried around a selection of very valuable signet rings to give to his male friends?"

"He was wearing it because his wife had given it to him – probably as an engagement present. Orr cast covetous eyes on it and so Searle gave it to him."

"What are the initials engraved on the ring?"

"R and B."

"And the Christian names of the Searles?"

"C and B," Keen answered reluctantly.

Drew leaned back in his chair, said nothing.

"It could have been a family ring. Perhaps it was her grandmother's and she did not want the initials altered because of the emotional association."

"When I started in the force, there was a sergeant of long service whose constant refrain was, 'Fit the theory to the facts, not the facts to the theory.' He was dead boring, but dead right."

"I know I'm assuming one or two things, but when everything else fits, surely that's justified?"

"Is there anything that does fit?"

"We know, as you said, that Searle started life under every disadvantage. So he's had to fight hard and long to get where he is. That probably says he prefers the end to the means. At one stage of his career, he met Berenice Ambrose, the daughter of the man who started and virtually owned the Aylton Shipping Company. There's no quicker way of promotion than marrying the chairman's daughter, so that's what Searle set out to do.

"But he was a homosexual at a time when homosexuality, for men, was a criminal offence. So that side of his life had to be kept under total cover from everyone, not just his fiancée who, if she'd had any inkling of that side of his life, would have declared the marriage a no-no and made certain her father gave him the hard push from the company.

"He sailed aboard the *Slecome Bay*, probably for business reasons, and met Orr. An attraction formed virtually immediately and, on Searle's part, became so strong that when Orr made a point of admiring the signet ring, he gave it to him despite the fact it may well have been his engagement present. He'd hoped the relationship had gone unnoticed, but a cargo ship is too small a community, even when a few passengers are carried, for anything to go unnoticed. And one night Orr barged into Noyes in the passenger accommodation which confirmed what Noyes had already suspected . . ."

"Are you claiming Noyes has blackmailed Searle ever since then?" Drew asked impatiently. "And that recently his demands had become too excessive to be allowed to continue? Blackmail requires good cause if it's to be effective, but homosexuality was no longer a criminal offence toward the end of the sixties."

"He wouldn't have wanted his wife to know."

"After several years of marriage, his wife may well have gained a good idea of what was what, but decided to accept the situation. And in this present age, especially in politics, there are those who would see it as an advantage."

"I haven't quite finished, sir."

"Then hurry it up."

"A homosexual relationship now isn't cause for blackmail, even if it took place at a time when it was illegal, and his wife may have closed her mind to what she knows – quite a lot of women do remain married to husbands they accept are bisexual . . ."

"Then where's the point in trying to say it's blackmail money?"

"Searle was being blackmailed not for his sexual orientation, but because he murdered Orr."

Drew started at him with an astonishment that turned to annoyance. "There's a point at which an imaginative approach changes into a bloody stupid one."

"The findings of the pathologist who carried out the PM on Orr were that he had died from drowning, but had also suffered a fractured leg and severe bruising, consistent with having been thrown overboard by the collision, plus a further injury to the back of the head, caused by something round of small diameter. It was assumed that the force of the collision had caused him to strike his head against a stanchion before he fell overboard. What was never explained was why he was out on deck, naked.

"At the moment of collision, he was in Searle's cabin. Whether standing, sitting, or lying in the bunk, he was thrown onto the deck and suffered a broken leg. So Searle had in his cabin an injured man, incapable of moving under his own steam, in circumstances which, if exposed, would make it all too obvious what had been going on and must bring an end to the engagement and all the consequences to flow from that. It seemed his future had suddenly blacked out. But if Orr were pushed through the port—"

"How big were the portholes in the passenger accommodation?"

"I don't know."

"It's a pity you didn't consider it necessary to find that out before you started propounding extravagant theories."

Drew had the typical senior's ability to identify a minor flaw when he didn't want to accept the conclusion, Keen thought angrily. "I'll try to find that out, sir."

Eleven

Keen telephoned the Aylton Shipping Company's head office and asked to speak to Benson. There was a brief wait before Benson said: "An astonishing coincidence, Mr Keen. I was just about to phone you. Do we consider the possibility of telepathy?"

"Why not? . . . What were you going to tell me?"

"That I am working on your request."

Keen was momentarily nonplussed since he had not yet put his question.

"I'm afraid it's going to take some time yet to complete, but rest assured it will be with you as soon as possible."

He remembered he'd asked for the names of ports to which the *Slecome Bay* had sailed in order to establish whether she had frequently docked where the drug trade was rampant. If he was correct and the money had nothing to do with drugs, such information was now irrelevant. Would it be more tactful to say so – leaving Benson to realise his work had been a waste of time – or allow the other to continue in the belief that what he was doing remained important? He decided on the latter course. "Thanks for all the work you're doing."

"I am happy to be of assistance."

"Mr Benson . . ."

"Yes?"

"You've made me hesitant to ask a further favour."

"But you will try to overcome such hesitancy?" A quick chuckle.

"I need to know the size of the portholes in the passenger accommodation of the *Slecome Bay*. You said she'd been scrapped, but I'm wondering if there's a chance you have plans or specifications?"

"I very much doubt it. The company has never had a ship built, but has always bought on the open market." A dry cough. "Rather on the principle of buying a second-hand car because then the major depreciation is borne by the original owner."

"Would it be any good getting on to whichever company first owned her?"

"You could always try. But tell me, how accurate do you have to be? Do you need the exact measurements or will an estimate do? My reason for asking is a practical one. The company has a policy that after a certain number of years' service in the office, an employee and a relative are granted a trip at sea on one of the ships in the fleet. I happened to sail on the *Aspart Bay*, which was a sister ship of the *Slecome Bay*, bought from the same company only a few weeks later, and there is no reason to suppose there would be any great difference in the size of the ports. Both my wife and I made our first flights when we went out to Suva to join her. That was exciting enough – once we had overcome our natural trepidation – but within two days of sailing, we'd seen flying fish, porpoises, a whale, a waterspout, and had been asked up to the bridge by the Captain . . ."

Keen patiently listened to the description of a voyage that might have taken place several years previously but was still sharp in the other's mind. Disembarkation in Wellington, for once not wet and windy, was finally reached. "So you can tell me what the portholes were like?"

"Dear me, that's why I started to tell you about the voyage, isn't it? I fear I must have bored you with my reminiscences."

"You have made me keen to go on a cruise."

"Cruising has unfortunately – in my opinion – become a very different experience from what I like to call 'being at sea'.

There are so many people and so much entertainment because passengers are not content just to sit and watch the water and the things that live in it and circle above it . . .''

That hint of a romantic soul beneath the dry and dusty exterior which Keen had first discerned was now in full flow. Unfortunately.

"There, I've verbally wandered again! But my wife and I so enjoyed our trip on the *Aspart Bay* that we saved to go on a cruise. It was a mistake and although we didn't dislike our second trip, I cannot say we wholeheartedly enjoyed it . . . I really must bring my mind to bear on the matter in hand! Our cabin didn't have the traditional small, round, brass-rimmed porthole. It was much more like a window except that one wound it up and down with a handle. Being well above the waterline, it did not, of course, have to be nearly as strong as a porthole lower down."

"What's your estimate of the size?"

"Perhaps two and a half feet wide and three feet high. You must allow that this is an estimate, but I venture to suggest I am not far wrong."

"Put it another way, could you have climbed through it?"

"Without a doubt. But I would never have considered doing so. The passenger cabins were outboard so to climb out would be to fall into the sea. I am not a strong swimmer."

Keen chuckled.

"Are you allowed to tell me, Mr Keen, why you are now interested in the size of the portholes, following your previous interest in the *Slecome Bay*'s ports of call?"

"We're pursuing a case which may have roots in the past. I'm afraid I can't go any further than that."

"I should not have asked."

"Thanks again for all your help. I'm sorry to be causing you so much work."

"It isn't all work. Going through the logbooks enlivens memories and even restores some."

As Keen replaced the receiver, Parr called out from three desks away: "There's the rugby club's annual party next Saturday. You're on, aren't you? Twenty quid the double ticket. A lively night guaranteed."

"If it's anything like last year's bash, it'll be a lot more than just lively."

"Seth and John maybe did go a little over the top with their full Monty action strip, but it was all good, clean fun."

"Is that what the girl thought who had her panties ripped off?"

"She took 'em off herself before she started shouting George had yanked 'em down. It was a joke."

"George didn't think so."

"He loses his sense of humour when he gets tanked up . . . I'll put you down for a ticket. And if Anne starts complaining, tell her I'm in charge of making certain things remain in bounds."

"Can you suggest anything more likely to keep her a mile away?"

"She's a good sport. She'll jump at the chance of a night out."

Possibly. But not with her husband. Keen stood. "D'you know if the Guv'nor's around?"

"No, but since everything's nice and peaceful, I doubt it."

The detective inspector was not in his room; Cain was in his. "Any idea where the great man is?" Keen asked.

"Either with the superintendent, or gone out; depends how long the talking downstairs goes on."

"Then I'll leave a note in his room."

"Telling him what?"

"The size of the portholes on the *Slecome Bay*. They were big enough to push a body through without any trouble whatsoever."

"And you reckon that news will make his day?"

Keen moved forward and sat on the edge of the desk.

104

"Why's he holding back? It's not like him. He's usually so sharp we're trying to catch up with him, not slowing down so he doesn't fall out of sight."

"You can't see it?"

"See what?"

"That you don't mix with a heavyweight like Searle until you can be certain you'll come out smelling of roses . . . With not enough to keep you busy, you think up a murder. If the Guv'nor accepts you could be right, he has to hold an investigation even though it occurred nearly forty years ago. There's no proof, only circumstances; a good chance there never will be any proof. So if Searle is questioned and decides he's irritated, insulted and harassed, he'll raise the roof and there'll be no way of facing him. Big, big black mark on the Guv'nor's record, the end to his ambition of striding around county HQ with enough silver braid to slow him down."

"You're suggesting he'll put ambition before justice?"

"You're still so naïve you can ask a question like that? Justice? What the hell does the word mean? Ask A Division. Last year, they all spent hours of unpaid overtime trying to nail the bastard who'd raped at least three women, one of whom committed suicide, only to have the case thrown out of court by the judge on procedural grounds. Ask the bloke who's beaten up and hospitalised, and then in court hears his assailants given nothing more than suspended sentences because they've had unfortunate childhoods. Ask the villains on the Costa del Sol who can't be extradited for the crimes which have made them millionaires."

"Life's not perfect. But surely it's our job to do the best we can to make it as good as it can get? We shouldn't hold back because we think someone may make nonsense of all we've done."

"You'd best quit this job before it quits you if that's how you think."

Keen slid off the desk. "I'll leave the note on his desk and hope he thinks differently."

Cain fiddled with a pencil. "You're pushing very hard."

"So?"

"You're pushing very hard."

"Is that a hint I should ease off?"

"And suffer a sermon from you about doing our duty? I've better things to do."

"Like working out how to avoid trouble?"

"Your mouth is going to get you into even bigger trouble than your bloody fool ideas," Cain said angrily.

He was probably right, Keen decided.

Convinced he had been summoned to the DI's room because Cain had lodged a complaint, Keen braced himself for a rough passage. He was surprised by Drew's mild: "Grab a seat."

He moved a chair and placed it in front of the desk, sat.

"I've read your note. The estimate of the size of the porthole is from memory, so we have to treat it with considerable caution."

"Benson sounds the kind of person who's as exact as he can be and if he's not very certain, says so."

"Can one judge a person from his voice over the phone? . . . This case has become rather like trying to catch a cloud. There's form, but where's the substance to hold onto? If Noyes was the victim of a straight hit-and-run, we're grasping at nothing."

"The cash in the deed box is fact."

"The assumption that it's black is theory."

"Where would a man like him find a hundred and sixty-two thousand quid?"

"From time to time, someone who's been living at a low level dies and then it's discovered he was comparatively wealthy."

"Who would have to have been a miser who found some

way of making the money, like playing the stock market. We've not found anything to suggest Noyes was in the market, property, or whatever; and his only banking was a building society account which has never had much in it. Moreover, he certainly wasn't a miser judging by the female company and the expensive cruises."

"The point I'm making is that we cannot prove the money was black."

There could be no arguing with that.

"And if it wasn't black, we are almost certainly not looking at two murders, one of which took place years ago. However, since we can't say for certain it wasn't black, a suspicion of murder is raised and it's our job to try to determine whether or not that suspicion is justified . . . In your opinion, in order to do this what should our next move be?"

"To see what we can learn from Mr Searle."

"In other words, if he threw the injured steward overboard to his death and, having been blackmailed since then, decided to have his blackmailer murdered. He's not going to say anything useful until he's officially questioned and placed under pressure, is he?"

"It's very unlikely. Difficult to see conscience affecting him."

"To pressure a man in his position is rather like baiting a tiger – one needs very stout bars between the two of you. Without proof, there are no bars."

Keen expected Drew to continue by saying that until there was proof, Searle would not be questioned.

"So things will have to be done very, very carefully in order not to let the tiger know it's being baited. Normally, I would speak to him with Sergeant Cain as backup – the more eminent the man, the more he demands his eminence be recognised – but then he'd not accept the call as little more than a formality. So here's how we'll play it. You will make contact and arrange a meeting; at that, you'll explain we're trying to find out about Noyes's background because he's left property and money and no named heir and we've been asked to try and find one; even knowing where he lived before he moved to this area would help. You'll point out how stewards have a habit of being over-loquacious, believing it may ensure a better tip, and so he might have mentioned that he lived in Hull, Doncaster, wherever, information which would give us a start. But shy away from any mention of Orr. It'll take tact and common sense, but use both and keep him friendly."

"If I'm to forget Orr, it doesn't sound very promising."

Keen waited, but Drew nodded to show the meeting was finished. He left and as he walked back to the general room, remarked to himself that Cain couldn't have been more wrong – Drew was merely cautious. And when all was said and done, he'd be a fool if he were not.

Parr looked up from his desk. "I forgot to mention that the twenty quid includes one drink each at the bar. After that, it's cash on the nail."

"I'll have a word with Anne." He crossed to the table by the noticeboard and picked up the local telephone directory.

"Assure her there'll be no panty-pulling."

"You guarantee that?"

"Of course not. If some of the lads get really tanked up, anything can happen. But tell a woman what she wants to hear and she's happy."

Keen sat, turned the pages of the directory and found the entry he wanted. C. Searle, Mierton Manor, Little Pressley. He dialled the first of three numbers.

"Mr Searle's residence," said a man in a heavily accented voice.

"I'd like to speak to Mr Searle. Detective Constable Keen, Clunford CID speaking."

"Who?"

He repeated his name and rank.

"Please to wait."

A minute passed before a woman said: "Yes?"

"Is that Mrs Searle?"

"Who wants to know?"

He again repeated his name and rank. "Is your husband at home, Mrs Searle?" he asked, assuming that only the lady of the house would speak with such rude authority.

"He is not."

"I need to have a word with him."

"About what?"

"To ask whether he can help us in an investigation. Can you tell me when he'll be at home?"

"I cannot." The connection was cut.

He replaced the receiver. "I'll bet she's never had her pants pulled off at a dance."

"Invite her along and promise her she could strike lucky."

Half an hour later, the phone, now on Barrat's desk, rang. Barrat lifted the receiver, listened, said: "One moment, please." He put his hand over the mouthpiece. "For you, Mike. She didn't give a name, but from the sound of her, she's no cuddly blonde."

Keen crossed the room and took the receiver. "Detective Constable Keen speaking."

"My husband will see you at ten a.m. tomorrow."

"Thank you for phoning, Mrs Searle . . ." But she had not waited to hear his thanks. He replaced the receiver. "Rude bitch!"

"A close friend?"

"How did you guess?"

Twelve

M ierton Manor, approached through a stone gateway with elaborate wrought-iron gates and along a four-hundred-yard drive bordered by ancient, majestic oaks, was not a grand house in the sense that it awed a visitor; on the contrary, its four spiral chimneys, moss-patched roofs, beautifully matched stone walls, and leaded windows possessed a quiet charm that made the visitor view it as no more than a home, if an unusually large one. It had a chequered history. Built in 1568, extra rooms had been added in 1608 by a direct descendant of the first owner whose wife produced fourteen children, only two of which died in infancy. In the eighteenth century an east wing which destroyed the proportions of the whole had been built; in 1803, this had been demolished. In the Great Chamber on the first floor was a four-poster bed, richly columned and carved, in which the Prince Regent had slept. The plaque on the wall which recorded that fact did not add that a contemporary report mentioned he had been accompanied by a certain Mrs Fitzherbert.

Keen drove slowly between the oaks, each one an arboreal galleon, and wondered whether to live amidst such beauty was to deflect many of the darts of misfortune which life so often threw? Would any wife leave here for no reason other than that she refused to understand her husband?

A man in white coat, black tie and striped trousers, his features having an oriental cast, opened the heavy wooden door that was striated by time. Filipino, he judged. The hall was not the cavernous space he had expected, with no basis for such expectation other than imagination, but it was large enough comfortably to house two full suits of armour, four patterns of flintlock pistols on the walls, an open fireplace that could comfortably have roasted a baron of beef, several solid wooden chairs that looked uncomfortable, and an oval oak table that must take several men to lift. He was ushered into what he would have called the sitting room, but had little doubt it possessed a less bourgeois name. Lacking much knowledge of antiques, he was still certain that the two display cabinets containing delicate figurines, beautifully inlaid desk, longcase clock, and large carpet glowing with colour were of the highest quality and worth a great deal of money; by the same token, the four oil paintings, each in a very ornate frame, might look dreary, but were probably by minor, or even major, masters.

When Berenice Searle entered, he said a polite "Good morning", but she merely nodded as she crossed to a chair and sat. Her face was long and thin, her nose aquiline, her lips sparse, her mouth straight. He thought she probably found difficulty in even *saying* "passion".

"My husband is not here," she said, her voice nasal, high pitched, and full of indifference.

He waited for her to explain why Searle was not keeping the appointment, but it became obvious she saw no necessity to do so. Courtesy was an unnecessary luxury. "Perhaps I could arrange another time to speak with your husband?"

"I have no idea whether or when it will be convenient."

"I do need to have a word with him."

"I have explained the position."

It was a pity that Drew, whose temper was short, had not decided to take charge of the questioning. It would have been interesting to see if he managed to remain polite.

The door opened and the manservant entered, a cordless phone in his right hand. He crossed to where she sat. "The señor."

"How do you expect me to talk to him when you're holding the phone?"

He handed it to her.

"Yes?" She listened. "Very well, Ric." She lowered the phone and faced Keen. "My husband wishes to speak to you."

It would have afforded him great pleasure to reply that he couldn't speak to her husband all the time she was holding the phone. He crossed the carpet, took the phone from her, and even managed to thank her as he did so. "DC Keen here, Mr Searle."

"I'm sorry I'm not at home to meet you as arranged. Unfortunately, I had suddenly to drive up to the office because my job bears witness to the truth that time and tide wait for no man."

Keen was so surprised by Searle's friendly manner that he did not immediately reply.

"Are you still there?"

"Yes, Mr Searle. Of course I quite understand. Can we fix another time?"

"When would suit you?"

"The sooner, the better."

"How about ten o'clock tomorrow morning?"

"That would be fine."

"I'll note that down and should it seem necessary, I'll try to understudy Canute and order the tides to wait." There was a quick chuckle. "And now will you be kind enough to ask my wife to have another word with me?"

He crossed to where she sat, held out the phone. "Your husband would like to talk to you."

She stood, took the phone from him, left the room.

Pas devant les domestiques. A couple of minutes later, the door opened and the manservant beckoned him out. There was no sight or sound of Mrs Searle, but as he crossed the hall and came level with another room to his right, the air seemed suddenly to cool. He guessed that she had gone in there.

* * *

113

Keen reported to Cain that Searle had not been at home, but had arranged a meeting for the following day. "He surprised me because over the phone he was so friendly."

"Become mixed up in politics, hasn't he? All smiles even while he's putting his boot into your goolies."

"It made such a contrast to his wife. 'Bow, bow, ye lower middle classes! Bow, bow, ye tradesmen, bow, ye masses.'"

"What are you on about?"

"Gilbert and Sullivan."

"Can't stand 'em . . . There's two reports come through from Birmingham about the Audi."

"Any joy?"

Cain shuffled through the papers and files on his desk, swearing when he failed to find what he sought. "I know I put the goddamn things here . . ." He picked up two faxes which had been clipped together, passed them across.

Keen read. Despite the extensive fire damage, Vehicles had established that the car had suffered damage to its nearside front wing and the headlamp had been smashed – a few slivers of glass had been recovered and were on their way for comparison tests; no other meaningful traces had been found. He looked up. "That was the car."

"How about waiting for the results of the comparison tests before shouting?"

"'Whatever you do, do cautiously, and look to the end.'"

"Bloody Gilbert again?"

"I can't remember. Sounds more like Asquith."

"Instead of showing your ignorance, how about getting back to work?"

Keen read the second fax, which was from the Newcastle police. Information had been received (i.e., a nark had been whispering in the hopes that his information would be worth a few pounds) that Ed Chambers, an expert wheel who worked for the heavy mobs when the money was right, had started spending like there was no tomorrow and boasting he'd done a clean job down south. Nothing more was known at the moment, but inquiries were in progress . . .

Cain said: "Don't start telling me that there's the driver of the grey estate."

"But everything fits."

"Does it? You know more than they tell us? When did he start spending heavily?"

"Obviously, recently."

"Recently like what? One day, four days, a couple of weeks? What does 'down south' mean?"

"South of London."

"Where does it say that?"

Recognising the futility of arguing, Keen was silent.

"There've already been two reports in this morning of shoppers getting their handbags dipped in the High Street – looks like we're entertaining a visiting team. Bring 'em in before they do real harm and nick the mayoress's diary."

It was so easy to issue the order, Keen thought. Pickpockets more often than not worked in threes – one to steal, one to take whatever had been stolen and disappear, one to block any attempt to head off the second person – and it needed trained eyes and time to pick them out from the ordinary shoppers; if he succeeded in doing so, it would almost certainly be only after a long time and the very act of identification might alert them so that, laughing all the way to wherever they'd stored the loot, they would vanish before he could summon help to arrest them. Success in crime detection had been defined as thirty per cent skill, thirty per cent sweat, and forty per cent luck. He wasn't feeling lucky.

He stepped into the small hall and handed Laura the gift-wrapped box.

"What a lovely surprise!"

"For a lovely lady."

"Isn't that a little corny?"

"I can only plead it was meant well." She could surprise him. Sometimes a sharp edge to her character unexpectedly surfaced.

"Then you're forgiven. I'll call Sandra."

Pray don't bother, he silently said.

"Dra," she called out.

There was no response. "I suppose she's wearing headphones and listening to the noise that's called music these days; sometimes when I hear it, I think I'm so out of touch I must be a hundred years old."

"If it weren't too corny, I'd say you never look a day over twenty."

"You don't improve!" She smiled. "Go on through. I'll be with you in a minute."

In the sitting room, he picked up and read the previous day's copy of the *Daily Telegraph* until he heard her and Sandra come down the stairs.

He wished Sandra a good evening.

"Where's the present?" she asked.

"Mr Keen wished you good evening," Laura said.

"I heard."

"Then what do you say?"

"I want to open the present."

"It was given to me." Laura looked at Keen. "What does one do?"

Ignore all the politically correct softies and administer a smart tap on the behind in the hopes that that would inculcate some manners. "Sooner come between a dog and its bone than between mother and daughter."

"You're a great help!"

"I have a developed sense of self-preservation."

"Very obviously!" Laura turned to Sandra. "It's my present, but if you like, you can open it." She handed the package over.

Sandra pulled impatiently at the satin bow. "I hope it's nice."

116

"Presents are always nice."

"One of the ones Father Christmas gave me was stupid."

Laura said to Keen: "The colour pencils were of such poor quality that the leads kept breaking when one tried to sharpen them. She was terribly disappointed."

Sandra tore the paper free. "Chocolates!"

He said to Laura: "The last time I was here, I gained the impression truffles were a favourite."

"And my downfall!" She saw Sandra pull up the lid of the box. "Just one."

"Why?"

"Because they're so very rich that you can't properly enjoy more than one."

"I can."

"Just the one."

"I want two. Please, please."

"Do you promise to clean your teeth extra well and go to bed as soon as you've had a second one?"

Sandra hurriedly put a truffle in her mouth, then brought out a second one and held it in her hand.

"Manners, love. You should offer them to Mr Keen before you help yourself."

"He doesn't like them," she said through a mouthful of truffle.

"You can't possibly know until you've asked him."

Very unwillingly, Sandra held out the box.

"I do like them, but I won't have one just now, thanks," Keen said.

She very quickly withdrew the box.

"And what about asking me if I'd like one of my own present?" Laura asked.

She hesitated.

"Maybe I'll be like Mr Keen and have one later. Put the box down on a table so that the mice can't get at it."

"There aren't any mice."

117

"Right now, there's one very hungry one."

She looked at her mother, finally did as told. She put the second truffle in her mouth.

"When you can speak, say goodnight and then go on up to bed."

"I don't want to."

"Remember your promise."

"I'm not tired."

"Don't be difficult. You were such a nice, helpful girl earlier on."

"I want him to read to me."

"I'm sure he's too tired."

She faced Keen. "Are you?"

"I'm afraid I am rather worn out."

"I don't think you can read."

"Sandra! Enough of that," Laura said and for once there was authority in her voice. "Now go on upstairs. And do your teeth really well."

Sandra stamped her way out of the room and up the stairs.

"It's been a bit of a difficult day," Laura said.

For his money, every day was a difficult one when Sandra was about.

In the hall, he said: "When shall we two meet again?"

"Certainly not in thunder and lightning because they frighten me. When would you like?" Laura said.

"As soon as possible."

"Friday?"

"That's an aeon away."

"Mike, as I've said before, I just don't want to rush things. It's not very long since Ralph died . . . He always told me that if he died first, I mustn't dress in widow's weeds, but I can't help feeling . . ." She became silent.

"Disloyal?"

"If you like."

"Then we don't rush things."

"Has anyone told you you are a very nice person? So goodnight, nice person." She kissed him on the lips. But when he pressed his more firmly against hers, she moved back.

"How about if I bring a bottle of wine and duck in orange?"

"Isn't that rather extravagant?"

"My family always did have champagne tastes and beer incomes."

He left, walked briskly along the pavement to where he had parked his car. As he settled behind the wheel, he told himself that she would understand how, when the stress of work built right up, a man had to have a jar or two with his mates; she wouldn't create hell when he came home a little late. As he drove off, he assured himself she'd be sympathetically understanding, not angrily censorious, if he returned just a little cheerful. And despite that very occasional sharp edge to her character, she wouldn't believe her loyalty was being spurned . . . Pity about Sandra, but a touch of quiet discipline would civilise her . . .

He had just passed the old quarry – production of ragstone had ceased many years before – when he braked to a sudden stop, causing a following car to swerve; the blast of horn told him what the other driver thought of his competence. As he stared at the road, illuminated by the headlights, he wondered if anyone really understood how a mind worked? How could he not have realised until now the significance of Laura's call to Sandra when he'd first arrived? He made a U-turn, drove back to Sibton Avenue. He double-parked, crossed to the front door, rang the bell.

After a while, Laura called out: "Who is it?"

"Mike."

"What do you want?"

"To ask you something." He could imagine the nature of the questions that were racing through her mind and was unsurprised when there was no immediate response. Finally, there were the sounds of bolts being withdrawn and she opened the door. She wore, he was quick to notice, a dressing-gown over pyjamas.

"I'm not going to ask you in, Mike."

"I don't expect you to." Hope was a different matter. "What I need to know is why, when I arrived, you called out 'Dra' to Sandra?"

"Is that a serious question?"

"Far more serious than you can realise."

"Surely the answer's obvious? When Sandra was younger, she couldn't manage her name in full, so she called herself Dra."

"A shortening of her full Christian name?"

"Of course."

"I'll bring you another box of truffles on Friday in gratitude."

"For heaven's sake, in gratitude for what?"

"Persuading my sluggish brain to add another piece of the jigsaw."

"What jigsaw?"

"One I've been trying to put together at work . . . Am I permitted to kiss you goodnight?"

"You've already done so. Till Friday, Mike." She smiled at him before she closed the door. He heard the bolts being pushed home.

Thirteen

The door of the DI's office was ajar, so Keen entered without knocking.

"Yes?" said Drew.

"I was reminded last night of something that's important, sir. People are often called by their pet names."

"Am I supposed to be astounded by such percipience?"

"And the pet name is often a shortening of the Christian name."

"My time is limited and, I like to think, too valuable to have it wasted by listening to the obvious."

"As the sarge will have told you, when I was at Searle's place yesterday, he phoned to apologise for not being there. When his wife answered the call, she called him 'Ric'. That's usually a shortening for Roderick or Richard, but as his name's Cedric, it's odds on it's a pet name. The only problem with that is, she doesn't strike me as the kind of person to use pet names. Still, perhaps it's a habit started when they were engaged and the grass was very green. It's only later on that it starts to brown, isn't it?"

"There is a reason for all this waffle?"

"She calls him Ric."

"So you said."

"Which provides the initial R."

"As an example of the obvious, that can hardly be bettered."

"D'you remember the signet ring, sir? On it, engraved probably after the ring was made, are the initials R and B."

Drew put down the letter on the desk, leaned back in his chair. "I had forgotten . . . Do we know the wife's Christian names?"

"Berenice Isolde. The first could be shortened to Nice, but what name could be more inappropriate?"

"Leave your inane comments at home."

"Yes, sir."

Drew rubbed his chin. "How do you suggest the ring came into Noyes's possession?"

"Searle was instantly attracted to Orr on the *Slecome Bay*; Orr, of an acquisitive nature, suggested that a present of the signet ring would cement a wonderful friendship. It wouldn't have been a good fit because their fingers were almost certainly of different sizes which is why, when Orr was thrown about by the collision, the ring slipped off his finger and lodged somewhere where it was not immediately visible. Searle, deciding there was only one way of escaping the potentially disastrous situation in which he found himself, knocked Orr unconscious and bundled him through the port, not noticing, as he was under very great strain, that the ring was not on the other's finger. At some stage before the ship limped into port, Noyes cleaned out the cabin and found the ring. He'd last seen it on Orr's finger and so he now knew Searle was the passenger whom Orr had previously been visiting. At this point, I'd guess he decided to sell the ring for what it would fetch. But when Orr's naked body was found, Noyes realised that Orr must have been in Searle's cabin at the time of the collision, so how come he had fallen into the sea? There was only one answer and blackmail became a much more profitable possibility."

"An imaginative reconstruction."

"Do I take the ring and see if Searle identifies it?"

"First, you find out if he calls his wife a pet name in their lighter moments, making it far less likely that B stands for Berenice. But don't ask him directly, or even indirectly. Not only would the question arouse further curiosity which we don't need at the moment, to answer might embarrass him. Some pet names make one want to puke. Take things very, very quietly."

It was unusual, Keen thought, for the other to want an investigation carried out in slow motion.

As he approached Mierton Manor for the second time, he admired the setting as much as, perhaps more than, before. He envied the Searles their luck in being able to live amidst such timeless beauty, but there was no corrosive jealousy in that envy. He hoped there would always be those rich enough to maintain such homes. The past was as important as the future.

A woman, youngish, very attractive in a Far Eastern style, greeted him. Probably the wife of the manservant, he decided. She showed him into the same room in which he'd been before. He expected to be left waiting, but Searle hurried into the room almost immediately. The quintessential English gentleman of tradition, was Keen's immediate judgement – all traces of deprived youth vanished. Searle was just over six feet tall and broad shouldered; his handsome features suggested warm interest touched with humour, but there was a hint of steel; his pepper and salt hair was carefully cut and trimmed to hide any thinning; his well-proportioned body was clothed in a two-thousand-guinea suit, perhaps from Anderson & Sheppard, and his highly polished shoes had to come from Charles Jourdan. But what marked him more than anything else was the air of quiet certainty that was almost a sense of superiority, but not quite because he saw no need to prove himself superior.

He shook hands with a firm, but not challenging, grip. "Morning. Very sorry about yesterday, but I simply had no option other than to miss my appointment with you. I can't claim the fate of the nation hung on my being in London, but a couple of important matters certainly did . . . May I offer you coffee?"

"I had some earlier, thanks all the same."

"Do sit." Searle picked up a large, chased silver box. "A cigarette?"

"I managed to give up smoking some time ago."

"Wise man. I wish I had the same restraint." He opened the box, brought out a cigarette and lit it. He sat. "I must warn you that my wife and I have to leave here in half an hour's time, but until then I'll be happy to give you any assistance I can."

"Thank you, sir. To be honest, coming here is a bit of a long shot. What's happened is that an elderly man called Reginald Noyes was knocked down and fatally injured by a car not far from his house in Kingsholte and the car didn't stop so we're trying to identify the driver."

Searle drew on the cigarette, exhaled, tapped it on the polished ashtray even though there had not been time for ash to form. "Very unfortunate. But I don't understand how I might be able to help you do that."

"Of course, you can't. But we are also having to try to trace a relative so that all the usual things can be carried out, such as arranging the burial. And then we also have to know if there is an heir."

"He has a sizeable estate?"

"As far as we can find out, just the house and a small sum in a building society."

"Surely his will names his heir?"

"We've found no will and none of the local firms of solicitors drew one up – not even the people who handled the purchase of the house. And he doesn't seem to have had any friends who could tell us."

"No useful papers in the house?"

"No."

Searle smiled. "Forgive me. I must sound as if I were trying to teach you your job. That's what comes of having to provide

a solution to every problem that's presented to me at work . . .
It's sad to hear of someone who seems to have been virtually
alone in the world."

"It is, isn't it? So we're talking to anyone who may be able to
help us, even if, as I said earlier, it's a long shot."

"I think your coming here might well be described as a
misfire!"

"But you did know him?"

"What makes you suggest that?"

"You were on the *Slecome Bay* with him."

"I have no recollection of the fact." Searle stubbed out the
cigarette although it was only half smoked. "Are you sure of
what you say?" He took another out of the box.

"Amongst the papers there were in his house were records
of his trips and in one of them he noted that Mr Cedric Searle
was a passenger."

"The *Slecome Bay* . . . Yes, I remember now – I did sail on
her once."

"When she was in collision with the *Atoka*."

"So it was! . . . How extraordinary to have one's memory
jogged like this." He flicked open the lighter, took time
lighting the cigarette. "Was this unfortunate man aboard
on that trip?"

"He was a passenger steward."

Searle spoke slowly. "I seem to remember . . . Noyes. Was
he a butterball of a man, overweight and with a skin that
always looked shiny from sweat?"

"I'm afraid I never saw him, before or after the accident."

"If he was the person of whom I'm thinking, he had an
unfortunately obsequious manner. Of course, the line between
good and obsequious stewarding is a thin one . . . What if I am
correctly remembering Noyes?"

"He might have told you something about himself – like
where he was living, whether he had any brothers and sisters
and where they lived."

"Even if he did, after all these years I'm afraid it's most unlikely I'd remember the details. And without, I hope, sounding too stuffy, I discourage personal reminiscences – I find them either boring or embarrassing."

"It was just a possibility. I'm sorry to have bothered you." Keen stood. "Many thanks, sir, for taking the time."

"If I should remember anything that might conceivably be at all useful, I'll get in touch with you. Perhaps you'll tell me how best to do that?"

Keen brought out of his pocket one of the cards with divisional HQ's telephone number.

"I'll call Pedro to see you out," Searle said, as he took the card.

"Please don't bother. I can find my own way."

"Then goodbye, Constable."

"Goodbye, sir." Keen left. As he crossed the hall, he wondered if someone so friendly, so open, really could murder one man and plan the death of another . . . Thinking like a fool! He opened the door, which was even heavier than it looked, and stepped out. The best con-artist could make one regard him as a blood brother in five minutes flat. And Searle's personal history said that that hint of steel was no liar.

He drove westward for a mile, parked in a natural lay-by along a small lane and watched a herd of cows strip-grazing a twenty-acre field. If one were going to farm, his father had said, keep off cows. They had to be milked twice a day, or three times if one were very keen, seven days a week; they were as prone as humans to ailments; they produced waste in lake-like quantities and since the advent of cubicles and environ-mentalists, the disposal of that was a nightmare; they were frequent liars when it came to the declaration of their eager-ness to have sex; they could be more dangerous than bulls when they had calves to heel; they could find a way through a ten-foot-wide razor-wire fence . . . Cereals were the answer.

126

Then one had only to worry about lack of, or too much, rain, wind, crop circles, ramblers, earthborne and airborne diseases, the breakdown of the combine harvester at the precise moment when the clouds blackened . . .

An hour had passed since he'd left Mierton Manor. He started the engine, turned, and drove back. The front door was opened by Pedro. "The señor not here."

"That's OK. I'll have a quick word with you and your wife."

"Wife in Luzon with children."

"Then the young lady . . . ?"

"Clemente helps."

That he should be so lucky! Keen stepped inside.

"What you wish?"

"I meant to ask Mr Searle something but forgot. One of you may be able to tell me the answer."

He had the knack of getting on with people and gaining their confidence and it wasn't long before they were in a small, snug sitting room and Pedro was chatting freely and answering questions that would never have been put to his employers. The señor was normally a thoughtful employer, but he did have a temper and when annoyed it was best to keep well out of his way . . . Clemente came into the room. She agreed the señor was a good employer, if sometimes over-fussy about things being done exactly as he wanted. But then he paid well and provided them with a small car. And when her mother had been taken ill and for a while it had seemed she would not survive, he had said that if necessary she could fly to Davas and he would pay the fare.

Keen asked if Mrs Searle was equally as good an employer.

Her scorn was sharp. If he couldn't judge what kind of a woman the señora was, he was one very poor detective! She would never have offered to pay the fare home. She was a dried-up husk of rice. Nothing was ever right. If there was a big dinner party, she and Pedro would be working until midnight, but she still expected them to start first thing in the morning.

He commiserated with her. Sadly, there were employers who lacked the manners to consider their staff. It seemed odd that a couple could be so different in character. Still, as long as their marriage was happy . . .

Happy? She chewed up the word. What man could be happy married to such a woman? The señor was a saint to put up with someone so frigid throughout the day and no doubt even more so at night . . .

Pedro spoke in a language that Keen could not place – certainly, it wasn't Spanish. She replied, talking even faster and gesticulating. She turned to Keen. "He say we should not talk like this. I say, is truth."

He gently challenged her assertion that the marriage was a loveless one. When he'd visited the house previously, Mrs Searle had spoken to her husband on the phone, had called him by a pet name . . .

What was a pet name?

He tried to explain. People who used pet names were usually very fond of each other. If Mr Searle called his wife by one, this would confirm that appearances were deceptive and in the truth the two, like all happily married couples, loved each other . . .

It seemed he never called her anything but Berenice – a word Clemente had great difficulty in pronouncing.

"What makes you say he was nervous?" Drew asked.

"I'm certain he's normally a man who's very self-assured and precise. After I mentioned Noyes's name, he wasn't that. Took a long time to light a cigarette and his hand was shaking slightly . . ."

"Part of getting old."

"His hands weren't shaking at all earlier on."

"He wasn't lighting a cigarette."

"When I started talking about the *Slecome Bay*, he stubbed out the one he was smoking even though it wasn't half smoked, almost immediately lit another."

"According to some experts, the real danger in a cigarette is in the last half. He can afford to believe the experts."

"He wanted to know the size of Noyes's estate."

"The rich are always fascinated by other people's money."

"I reckon he was trying to find out if we'd uncovered a load of cash which had made us curious ... I'm certain that underneath he was becoming more and more nervous."

"An impression can be accurate only when the person concerned is not too impressionable."

"He told me he and his wife were leaving, so I waited until they'd gone and then returned and had a word with the two servants. They've never heard him call her anything but Berenice."

Drew said: "You didn't stop to think that by returning and questioning the servants, he'll know that your talk about trying to identify an heir was all crap?"

"I don't see that."

"Because you choose to keep your eyes shut."

"He may never hear I returned."

"If they're at all loyal, they'll tell him."

"But how else was I to find out what he called her?"

"Knowing you, I'm surprised you didn't forget what I said and ask him to his face. Another time, try the novelty of thinking before you act ... That's all."

Keen did not move.

"Well?" Drew snapped.

"What about the signet ring?"

"What about it?"

"Surely it's time to ask Searle if it's his, because if he identifies it, we'll know Orr was in his cabin that night."

"We could surmise he was, no more."

"But even that would take us forward."

"Up a blind alley?"

"Closer to solving two murders."

"Neither death has been proved to be murder."

"Then I'm not to show it to him yet?"

"It's your shout."

"Does that mean . . . ?"

"No more than I said."

Keen left, uncertain whether or not Drew's attitude reflected virtual disbelief in the case as presented.

A faxed report from Newcastle.

It had proved impossible to question Ed Chambers on the hit-and-run case because he had disappeared. To date, extensive inquiries had failed to provide any lead as to his present whereabouts.

"One half-witted constable asking a couple of questions and there's the end of it. They're not going to pull their fingers out for another force," Cain said scornfully.

"Judge others by your own standards?" Keen suggested.

Cain looked up and across the desk. "If you think you're being smart, you're bloody mistaken."

"Not for the first time. So where's Chambers? Disappeared to enjoy the Mediterranean sun, sea, sangria and sex, or six feet under?"

"Are you trying to raise another murder?"

"Why not? This one wouldn't be our problem."

"You're our problem. Clear off and leave me in some sort of peace."

Keen turned into an empty slot in the car park, under the nose of another car. He picked up the book, wrapped in coloured paper, stepped out of the car, locked the door, walked across to the main entrance of the hospital. One could not visit hospitals at relatively frequent intervals, as he had to do because of work, without understanding that life was never

settled and therefore every second of health should be sa-
voured. But how one put that precept into practice when one
was living a miserable life on one's own . . .

It seemed ironically fitting that as he began to cross the large
reception area, he should come face to face with Anne and
Judy. Judy giggled with pleasure and rushed forward to hug
him. "The doctor says I'm a very brave girl. Mummy's going
to make me some chocolate mousse, but not too much or I'll
be sick. What's that in your hand?"

"A present."

"For me?"

"For someone who's ill in bed. But now it seems I don't
know anyone who is."

"Give it to me."

"Manners, young lady," Anne said.

He handed Judy the parcel and in her eagerness she began to
tear the paper free. This recalled Sandra's unwrapping the
truffles . . . He jerked his mind forward. There were shadows
under Anne's eyes. "You look worn out."

"I've been very worried."

Her tone suggested he had not been. "So have I."

She looked away.

Judy pulled the last of the paper free and let it fall to the
ground.

"Pick it up and find somewhere to put it," Anne said.

Judy picked up the paper with her free hand. "I've read it,"
she said in a disappointed voice, before handing the book to
Anne and then crossing to a bin into which she dropped the
wrapping paper.

Anne looked down at the book. "This is what you'd
promised to read to her, but couldn't find the time to return
home and do so."

"In other words, a typical balls-up. But don't I get a mark
for good intentions?"

"Cancelled out by the poor execution, wouldn't you say?"

Judy, walking lackadaisically, returned.

He said: "The bookshop promised to change it if you didn't want it."

She brightened. "Then let's go now."

"We have to return to Aunty Fay's," Anne said.

"Is Daddy coming as well?"

"I'm afraid he's too busy." She took hold of Judy's hand and led the way outside.

The wind was gusting sufficiently to cause Anne suddenly to have to reach down to hold onto the hem of her skirt. He remembered the time, not long before their marriage, when they had been on top of the Devil's Dyke – a deep cleft in an otherwise rolling hill – and the wind had lifted up her skirt and, since no one else was around, she had not immediately moved to restrain it . . . Deserted men should be granted missing memories.

She came to a halt by the tired Fiesta they had bought second hand three years previously, inserted the key and unlocked the driving door.

"Suppose . . ." he began.

She said sharply, still holding the key in the lock: "This isn't helping someone and the longer it goes on, the more unsettling it'll become for her."

"I didn't plan it."

"Does that make a difference?"

"None. But as it's turned out the way it has, can't we at least go and have coffee together?"

"And a squishy doughnut with jam?" Judy said.

"There isn't time." Anne withdrew the key, opened the driving door, reached across the seat to unlock the passenger door, settled behind the wheel. "Hurry up, Judy."

"But, Mummy—"

"Get in the car."

When Judy was settled and secured by the seat belt, Anne started the engine, began to back.

"Hold it," he called out as a van came along between the lines of cars. As she turned her head to make out what was the problem, he became convinced she was struggling to keep back tears. Then whatever her words, her heart was not in tune with them. He banged on the window and she lowered it. "Let's give it another try?"

"And have to go through all this again?"

"If I promise things will be different?"

"If only I could rely on your promises, but you've proved I can't."

She turned the car and drove off.

Fourteen

K een was shown into the room by Pedro. Searle stood in front of the fireplace, his reflection in the large and ornately framed mirror revealing, despite the hairdresser's art, he was balding on the crown. He wore a white shirt, a neckerchief, a blazer, and light fawn flannels. Anyone for croquet? Keen thought. "Good evening, sir."

"You're becoming a regular visitor."

It had been said lightly, pleasantly, but Keen thought he caught an undertone that was neither. "I must apologise for that."

"No apology necessary. And before you tell me why you're here, will you have a drink?"

At that moment, a gin and tonic was more tempting than a raven-haired houri, but it was hardly sense to reveal such eagerness to a past chairman of the Police Authority. "Thank you, but I won't . . . I'd like to show you something and ask you if you recognise it."

"What exactly is this something?"

He took the small box out of his pocket, removed the lid, separated the tissue paper and lifted out the signet ring. He handed this across.

Searle visually examined it. "I've not seen it before." He passed it back.

He'd answered with careless confidence and Keen reluctantly accepted that he was probably speaking the truth. An unwelcome conclusion. If it had not been Searle's signet ring found in the cabin after the collision, his theory of what had happened that night was no more than a playing-card house, brought crashing down when an attempt was made to lay the final card.

The door opened and Berenice entered. She wore a twin set whose colour did not flatter her poor complexion and jewellery that highlighted the unsuitability of her wearing it, yet her sense of self-importance insulated her from any criticism. "Pedro has just told me that he is here again." She might have been referring to an annoying mendicant.

"Mr Keen has called to ask me something," Searle answered easily.

"This is becoming ridiculous. You must complain."

"I don't think there's any need to do that."

She faced Keen. "You have no right to continue to make a nuisance of yourself."

"When we're investigating a case, Mrs Searle, I'm afraid we often have to keep asking people questions. But we do try to cause as little trouble as possible."

"Without success. Why are you bothering us this time?"

"To ask Mr Searle if he could recognise a ring."

"What ring?"

He would have enjoyed telling her it was none of her business. He brought it out of the box.

"Let me see it."

He moved forward to hand it to her.

She stared down at it, her expression first one of surprise, then of an emotion difficult to interpret. She looked up and at her husband. "You've told him whose it is?"

"How could I?"

"You don't remember?" Her words were now encased in icicles.

"Should I?"

"That depends on whether you think a husband should remember the present his wife gave him before the marriage to mark their engagement."

Keen wondered if his sense of excitement was as obvious as was Searle's sudden consternation.

"Where was this found?" she asked.

"It was in the possession of Mr Noyes at the time of his death," Keen answered.

"Who?"

"Reginald Noyes. The man who was killed in a hit-and-run case very near his home." Keen was watching Searle, but the other's expression was now blanked.

"How could he possibly have come in possession of it?"

"We don't know."

Searle said: "I lost the ring my wife gave me nearly forty years ago so I find it virtually impossible to believe this could be the same . . ."

"I've just told you it is," she snapped.

"It may be very similar . . ."

"I remember the ring exactly."

"All I'm trying to say, my dear, is that time can confuse. Realistically, if that were the ring you gave me, it would be a minor miracle for it to reappear now."

"Miracle or not, it has."

"I really don't think you can be right."

"Get one of the magnifying glasses from the library."

Keen wondered if the word "please" had ever visited her vocabulary.

Searle left the room. She sat, placed the ring on the occasional table at her side, and stared directly in front of herself, her mouth set straight, making it very obvious that she would not welcome casual conversation.

If she had been in a tumbrel, he decided, pride would have kept her head high and stupidity would have prevented her understanding why she was being driven towards the guillotine.

Searle returned, handed his wife a magnifying glass. She picked up the ring in her left hand, studied it through the glass.

"Since," she said slowly and carefully, "you hesitate to accept my word, perhaps you will see for yourself."

"What exactly am I to look at?"

She made a sound which, had it come from a lesser lady, would have been called a snort of angry frustration. "You don't even remember that I had our initials engraved?"

"Yes, of course." He examined the ring. "You are quite right, my dear. There are our initials and this is my ring. How remarkable! Incredible would be a better word if one did not have to believe . . . Mr Keen, I have great reason to thank you."

He had sounded genuinely grateful. "I'm afraid the ring can't be released to you just yet," Keen said. "We'll have to retain possession for a while. And we shall have to ask you, purely as a formality of course, if you can provide independent proof of identity; a claim against an insurance company, perhaps, if it was insured?"

"Naturally it was," she snapped.

"Then you may have a record of that claim?"

"We won't have kept it after all this time," Searle answered.

"Is my word not sufficient?" she asked aggressively.

"It's all a question of rules and regulations, Mrs Searle. Independent evidence of ownership of stolen property which has been recovered has to be obtained wherever possible, even in a case like this where it's clearly unnecessary from any practical point of view."

Searle said: "Presumably, you now want the ring back?"

"Yes, please. I'll give you a written receipt."

He came forward and handed back the ring.

"When are we allowed to repossess our own property?" his wife asked.

"As soon as possible," Keen replied.

"That hardly answers my question."

"I'm afraid it's all I'm in a position to say at the moment." He placed the ring in the small box and folded the tissue paper around it. "One very odd aspect of all this – I suppose unaccountable would be a better word – is that Noyes should have retained possession of the ring." He began to write a brief receipt.

"Why is that odd?" Searle asked.

"Having stolen it, either directly or by finding it in the cabin and not returning it, one would have expected him to sell it at the first possible opportunity."

"It was not lost in a cabin," she said. "My husband lost it when he was staying at a hotel."

"It can't have been," Searle corrected her.

"I do not forget facts as readily as you do."

"But if I'd lost it in a hotel, how could a cabin steward have found it? It had to be when I was aboard."

"You told me it was when you were staying at a hotel," she persisted sharply. "And I can remember your writing to them asking them if it had been found."

"Then all I can suggest is that my brain was thoroughly scrambled, which wouldn't have been very surprising. Not only was there the shock of the collision and its immediate aftermath, I was trying to work out what to advise your father that would cause the fewest problems consequent to the loss of the *Slecome Bay* for several weeks whilst she was repaired. You'll remember that at the time, the company was faced with several problems, one of which was serious."

She was unimpressed. "I cannot understand how you could tell me you'd lost the ring in a hotel when now you say you couldn't have done." She stood; Searle did the same. She left the room.

Searle sat. "As you'll understand, the memory still hurts even after all these years and despite the unexpected happy ending. Ladies are very sentimental about such things."

Squeeze out all the sentiment of which she was capable, Keen thought, and she wouldn't be a gram lighter.

"Perhaps, Constable, we've reached the stage where it

would be an idea for you to explain the true reason for your questioning of my wife and me?"

"I thought I had."

"When you claimed you were trying to trace a living relative of Noyes?"

"That's right."

"How does the ownership of my signet ring help you do that?"

"Obviously, it doesn't. But when we came across it in his possession, there was reason to think it was probably stolen, which meant we had to try to identify the legal owner."

"During his time at sea, Noyes will have met hundreds of passengers. Have you traced each one and shown him the ring?"

When his wife had not only identified the ring, but proved her husband a liar, Keen had congratulated himself; he had forgotten that a wounded animal could be at its most dangerous. He racked his mind for an answer that would sound feasible. "It didn't seem necessary to go to such lengths. The ring was found in the deed box in which was a report of the collision between the two vessels and it seemed likely there was a direct connection."

"Then you have shown the ring to all the other passengers who were aboard the *Slecome Bay* on that voyage and are still alive?"

"We are in the process of doing so. Now, obviously, it won't be necessary to continue."

"As a matter of interest, how did you go about tracing the names of the passengers?"

"One of the company's staff was able to find an old passenger list."

"That presumably was Benson?"

"I think that was his name," Keen replied, wondering just how deep was the hole into which he'd dug himself.

"He mentioned you'd asked him to name the ports the

Slecome Bay had visited, but I don't remember his adding a passenger list – and I'm very surprised to learn that one still exists . . . Incidentally, I think I should point out that having taken a great deal of trouble to trace out the information you required, Benson is, somewhat naturally, dismayed that you've never asked him for it."

"It's down in my diary to phone him tomorrow. With the pressure of work we're under, Mr Searle, we can't always act in an individual case as quickly as someone might think we should."

"He also happened to mention that you'd specifically asked if I was in any way connected with the company. I'd be interested to learn what aroused this interest?"

Keen was silent.

"Staff are a source of information, whether in a large company or a small household, but there almost always is the problem of sorting out fact from fiction. I say 'almost' because if Benson rang me here to say the world would end in half an hour, I would go down to the cellars and open one of the four remaining bottles of sixty-one Mouton-Rothschild and drink it quickly to make certain there wouldn't be a drop left at the moment of nothingness. But if Pedro said the same thing, I would leave it where it is for two, or possibly three, more years for it to reach an ultimate perfection. Therefore, when Pedro said that yesterday you had returned here shortly after we'd left and, among other things, asked him if I called my wife by a pet name, I judged him to be either talking nonsense or I had misunderstood his English, which is easily done. Now I begin to think I was probably maligning him. Is that so?"

"I don't exactly remember what was said, but I am certain I never asked him that specific question."

"What were your interests?"

"I'm afraid that for me, everything about this house is interesting and that extends to the lives of the owners. I know it's a prurient curiosity . . ."

"Don't strain your imagination any further. You believed the ring was mine, but couldn't be certain because of the initials engraved on the inside of it. When you were first here, you heard my wife call me Ric over the phone; had I called her by a pet name which did not begin with B, you reasoned the ring might not have been mine after all . . . I will ask you again – what is the true reason for your questioning me?"

"We are investigating the death of Noyes."

"And you believe I was driving the car which ran him down?"

"I am certain you were not."

"Then what leads you to have any further interest in my life?"

"We have to check every possibility, however improbable."

"And no matter how improbable it may be, you are certain that in some way I am implicated in the death of Noyes?"

"I have never suggested that."

"It's what you haven't suggested that interests me. Why was your need to know what ports the *Slecome Bay* sailed to so short-lived? Was it because you learned I had been a passenger on her? Yet why should that interest you? Because of something you found in Noyes's possession which raised the possibility that Noyes's death might not have been an accident?"

"I cannot explain the course of our investigation."

Searle stood, crossed to the nearer window and looked out at the garden and the park beyond. "As you will know – since I make no secret of the fact – I was born into a world of back-to-back houses and outside privies. That makes it even sweeter for me when I stand here and look out at flowers, grass, and trees." He turned. "Can you appreciate that?"

"Of course."

"And also that one fights even harder to retain what one has than to attain something one wants?"

"It's possible."

"It's fact." He walked back to stand in front of the fireplace. "Were the egregious planners who haunt this country and try their best to destroy the countryside ever to decide to run a by-pass through the park, I would take every possible step to stop that happening." His voice hardened. "Do you understand that?"

"Yes. But I'm wondering why you've said it?"

"I'm sure you're intelligent enough to work that out . . . Pedro can show you out."

"I can find my own way as I did last time."

"Too much certainty can be a double-edged weapon."

Keen left.

Cain was smoking a pencil-thin cigarette. "Well?"

"I showed him the ring. He didn't recognise it."

"But you, naturally, decided he was lying?"

"I reckoned he was telling the truth."

"You're full of little surprises. So now you can get back to doing some useful work."

"His wife turned up when least wanted."

"What wife doesn't?"

"She said it was the ring she'd given him on their engagement and that gave his memory a million-volt shock. He then tried to make her agree she could be wrong, but she wouldn't know how to do that; in any case, she was furious he hadn't recognised the ring. So she made him get a magnifying glass and told him to look at the initials. In the end, he had to admit it was his, at which point she marched off, head held high. If you ask me, she'll be making his life hell for a long time to come."

"I didn't ask you."

"With her out of the way, he started asking questions."

"Like what?"

"What was my real interest in the ring?"

"What d'you tell him?"

143

"That we had to identify the true owner. So why did we think it had been stolen and from him; had we spoken to all the other passengers Noyes had met during his time at sea; how did we know who were the passengers on the *Slecome Bay*; as I'd asked Benson for a list of ports the ship had sailed to, why hadn't I bothered to get back to him for the answers?"

Cain let smoke trickle out of his nose. "You bloody blew things."

"Not really."

"No? Searle's now certain you reckon he's mixed up in Noyes's death."

"I made it clear we didn't think that."

"Then he's doubly certain. Is it any wonder that every sergeant has half a dozen ulcers when there are blokes like you eager to balls up everything? Weren't you told, on no account upset him?"

"I didn't."

"With you plodding around, he'd have to be thicker than an obelisk not to realise what was going on."

"I can't see how I could have put things more circumspectly."

"You can't, but a thousand and one others could."

"He had to be asked."

"Only by someone bloody fool enough to imagine a man in his position would set a contract."

"Remember his background. And it's because of his position that he did. If he were accused of murdering Orr, he'd lose his social standing even if he weren't found guilty and that would have his wife foaming. But if he didn't have Noyes quietened, the blackmail would climb so high he'd become skint. And it's pertinent that he said a man would fight even harder to keep what he has than to get what he wants."

Cain's cigarette had gone out. He laid it on the ash tray. "The Guv'nor's going to be singing your praises to the sky!

. . . Make out a full report and have it on my desk by this
evening."

Keen did not move.

"And do it now!"

"Just before I left, he told me that if ever planners tried to
put a road through his property, he'd fight them all the way."

"So?"

"It was a threat. A warning that if I carried on digging into
his past, he'd put a contract on me."

"Get out before you try to tell me that Cleopatra's invited
you to supper."

Drew, for once looking less than smart because there was a very
recently acquired dirt stain on the collar of his shirt, picked up a
sheet of paper from his desk. "Having read this, I reckon
Sergeant Cain is guilty of gross understatement when he says
your visit may cause problems." He read aloud. " 'Mr Searle
asked me how I knew who had been on the *Slecome Bay* when
she was in collision and I said that Mr Benson had given me a
passenger list . . .' " He put the paper down. "It didn't occur to
you that Benson would probably report to Searle that the police
had asked for a list of ports the ship had sailed to, but had failed
to get back to him to learn what he'd been able to find out, which
must arouse surprise? And that if you had in truth requested a
passenger list, he'd have mentioned that as well?"

"I had to give some answers in a hurry, sir."

"Which succeeded in convincing Mr Searle that you were
suspicious. Why didn't you ask Benson for the list of ports?"

One did not admit one had forgotten something so important.

"Thanks to your negligence, we face the possibility of an
official complaint."

"You did suggest I and not you or the sarge question him."

"Because I made the mistake of assuming you were sufficiently competent to do so."

Would Drew have managed any better in the face of Berenice Searle's arrogant rudeness? Much more likely he'd have said something inexcusably rude.

"Am I correct in understanding you claim you were threatened by Mr Searle?"

"Yes, sir."

"What precise form did the threat take?"

"He said that if planners ever tried to run a by-pass through his property, he would do anything and everything to prevent it happening."

"You conceive that to be a threat?"

"It came out of the blue and had no connection with anything said before; and it was more the way in which he spoke than the actual words."

"Sergeant Cain has suggested more than once that you have an imagination better suited to public relations than this job."

"But Searle admitted the ring was his."

"Quite . . . Very well."

As Keen stepped out of the room, he wondered what exactly that "Quite" had signified?

Fifteen

K een drove up to the garage doors, stopped. He'd forgotten to set the timer so that a light came on to suggest occupation and the house was in darkness, emphasising the loneliness which waited inside. After suffering the detective inspector's sarcastic annoyance, he wanted company. Did he turn back and see if any of the lads was in one of the usual pubs? A film? What was on, had the last showing started? He didn't know or really care . . . Laura had said Friday, but she would understand how loneliness could sweep over a person and she must be sympathetic, especially if he arrived with a packet of smoked salmon and a bottle of wine.

He backed onto the road, drove up to the T-junction and turned right. At the twenty-four-hour Sainsbury's, the salmon was easily chosen, but not the wine because of the large selection. In the end, he decided on one bottle simply because the label pictured a field of vines underneath a blue sky – he needed blue skies.

As he drove towards Richly Cross, he wondered what sort of a man Ralph Ellis had been? There were no photos of him downstairs so there was no way of trying to judge whether he had been roughly of the same age as Laura, smoothly handsome or pleasantly chunky, naturally cheerful or more inclined to reality, understanding of women's foibles or luckily indifferent to them. Her only mention of him had been to say he had had a good sense of humour. Whatever the man, his legacy was a regrettably strong sense of loyalty on her part.

He cleared Clunford and drove a couple of miles on the London road, then turned off into a lane, bordered by thorn hedges, which twisted its way through agricultural land; occasionally, the headlights picked up the glint of eyes and behind them the bulk of a cow – saved from loneliness by being one of the herd.

He entered Sibton Avenue from the south. Did he excuse his arrival an evening early by forgetting she had specified Friday? Or did he . . . He laughed at himself. This "inner" conversation was more suited to a young teenager, relatively new to the ways of life. As he braked to a halt, he was reminded of the inner conversations he'd had when lusting after a redhead at a time when he'd lacked the self-confidence to attract her attention away from an eighteen-year-old whose father had owned a Jaguar . . .

He locked the car and walked along the pavement, pack of smoked salmon and bottle of wine in the supermarket plastic bag. He came to a halt at the front door and rang the bell. There was no response. He rang again, depressing the bell for longer.

"Who is it?" a young voice called out from inside.

In the light of the nearest street lamp, he checked the number on the door to make certain he was not at the wrong house. "Mike."

"What do you want?"

"Is Laura there?"

"No."

"Who are you?"

"I'm not going to tell you."

A baby-sitter? Laura had originally told him she'd been unable to find one . . .

"Go away or I'll call the police."

She sounded scared; seeing him as a potential rapist? "I am the police," he said, trying to calm her fears.

"I will call them. The phone's here, in the hall."

It seemed obvious words alone would not convince her. His warrant card was at home, but even if he'd had it, how would he have persuaded her to let him show it to her? "I'm on my way." He turned and walked towards his car.

As he approached a rubbish bin, put out from one of the houses, he suffered the urge to throw the salmon and wine into it as a gesture of bitter disappointment. But he remembered what they'd cost.

Ambition often left Drew less content with life than he had a right to be. He knew he was a good policeman and generally recognised as such; he was married to a woman with a warm, serene nature who asked of him only that he remained faithful; she had a well-paid job so they were comfortably off; and they had two children who were sound in life and limb. Yet he seemed to lack the ability to enjoy to the full his good fortune.

He parked immediately beyond the bays reserved for senior officers who worked at county HQ and climbed out of the car into a strong wind which flicked the ends of his black hair against his eyes, causing him to blink. He'd intended to have his hair cut several days ago, but had not yet been able to find the time.

He crossed to the portico of the Regency-style building, went into the very large reception area – typically, the architect had set more store by appearances than function – and gave his name to the PC acting as receptionist. He climbed the three flights of stairs at a good pace and continued along a corridor to the offices of the Assistant Chief Constable (Crime). The attractive secretary in the outer office gave him a welcoming smile and the assurance that he wouldn't have long to wait. He sat at a low, glass-topped table and picked up a six-month-old copy of the county magazine. By unhappy coincidence, one of the articles was about Cedric Searle, detailing his many generous donations to charities, the hands-on help he and his wife were always prepared to give at the expense of their own free time . . . Pile the soft soap any higher, Drew thought morosely, and the paragon of virtue would suffocate.

A buzzer sounded. The secretary said he was to go through.

Offices were graded according to rank and Metcalfe's was slightly smaller and less generously furnished than the Chief Constable's. He had an avuncular manner which fooled only those who did not know him well. "Good to see you again, Frank." He came round the desk to shake hands. "Grab a seat." He indicated the comfortable chair which had been set in front of the desk, returned to his, sat, rested his elbows on the desk, raised his forearms so that his fingertips touched, and studied Drew over the triangle thus formed. "I thought it best to ask you if you could find the time to come here in order to sort out a potentially annoying problem."

Drew reflected that he hadn't been asked, he'd been ordered.

"Prevention is so much better than cure." Metcalfe was addicted to clichés. "You'll know, of course, what the problem is."

"I imagine, something to do with Mr Searle."

"The Chief Constable, who knows him well, has received a complaint from Mrs Searle to the effect that the police are harassing her husband."

"I hope he suggested she made her complaint through the usual channels?"

"Usual channels, Frank, are for usual people. If a past chairman of the Police Authority, who holds a high position both in business and politics, has the manners to mention something on the quiet rather than do so officially and raise a stink, one needs to be grateful, not censorious."

In the eyes of the law, all were equal, except those who were privileged.

"She complains that a young detective is constantly turning up at their house, rudely questioning her husband, and falsely accusing him. Is that possible?"

"DC Keen has spoken to both of them. He's assured me that he has always been respectful and has accused Mr Searle of nothing."

"Would you like to fill me in as to why it's necessary to question Mr Searle?"

Drew gave a résumé of the case.

Metcalfe, his arms now by his side, leaned back in his chair. "How would you describe Keen?"

"Efficient, intelligent, not afraid of work. Perhaps at times a little too active an imagination."

"I'd say his imagination often takes off into the stratosphere. His ideas in this case are bizarre, more especially when one considers Searle's position in life."

Which Metcalfe was doing all the time. But, as no doubt he would have been quick to say, it was a fool who jumped before he'd measured the drop. "It is fact that the injuries to Orr were never fully explained."

"Surely the authorities accepted that when someone falls over the side of a ship, the injuries he sustains are likely to be unusual?"

"There's the money in Noyes's deed box."

"A miser, who distrusted banks. That cash represents his life's savings."

"He doesn't seem to have been a saver. He owned a BMW and frequently went on luxury cruises."

"It is surprising how reasonably one can cruise these days. It's not like seventy years ago, you know."

Yes, he did know. "And there's the ring. It's very difficult to imagine how that could have come into Noyes's possession if not when both men were on the *Slecome Bay* – indeed, Searle agrees with that. But why didn't he shout very loudly at the time that he'd lost it since it was of great sentimental and financial value?"

"Can you be certain he didn't?"

"All he says is, he claimed under his insurance."

"Which doesn't answer the question. I must say, Frank, I'm surprised you've allowed things to get so far out of hand."

"I don't think they are, sir. I decided we had to conduct an investigation because there are several aspects to Noyes's case that indicate the possibility of murder rather than manslaughter or causing death by dangerous driving and as a consequence . . ."

"What are these aspects?"

"A grey Audi estate was stolen in Newcastle and a similar car was seen, on the day of Noyes's death, parked at a point where the driver had a clear view of his house. Again, the car seen driving away at speed immediately after Noyes was knocked down was a grey estate. A day or two later, Ed Chambers, a wheel up north, was spending money like it's going out of fashion and talking about doing a good, clean job down south."

"Has Chambers been questioned?"

"He's disappeared. Probably lazing around on a beach and laughing."

"Then we have a lot of theory, but very little fact. A hit-and-run that can as easily have been accident as murder and a forty-year-old drowning that was more likely to have been accident than murder. I have to say it again, Frank, I am very surprised that in the circumstances you have seen fit to pursue the matter to the point of upsetting someone in Mr Searle's position."

"The moment the possibility of murder was raised, it became my duty to investigate that possibility . . ."

"You may take it that I am conversant with an officer's duty," Metcalfe said, clearly annoyed.

"Yes, sir."

"How do you propose to continue from here?"

"I think we should wait for Chambers to be brought in and questioned before moving forward."

"I agree. Keep me fully informed. And make certain Mr Searle has no further cause to speak to the CC."

Drew left. As he made his way down the stairs, he silently cursed Keen because he had just earned a black mark and one didn't need too many of those to ruin any reasonable chance of promotion to the upper ranks; as he reached the reception area, he silently cursed Berenice Searle for presuming that her husband's and her social and financial position should insulate them from pressures the ordinary person had to suffer; as he settled behind the wheel of his car, he silently cursed life which guaranteed much to the few and little but trouble to the many.

Back at divisional HQ, he called Cain into his room. "I've just had the ACC breathing fire down my neck because of Keen's ham-fistedness."

"I've always said . . ." Cain began.

"Then there's no need to say it again. Until Chambers is pulled in, questioned, and gives us something definite to work on, Searle is out of bounds. Say that to Keen loud enough for him to hear it."

"I did try to tell him . . ."

"Not vigorously enough."

It wouldn't have made any difference, Cain thought. The present-day youngsters had no respect for the natural order.

A report was received from the forensic laboratory – the glass found in the road matched the glass from the broken head-lamp of the burned-out Audi.

"Then like I kept saying, that was the car, Sarge, which means . . ." Keen was cut short.

"It means," Cain said, "that nothing's changed."

"If the driver was on a joy ride, the car would just have been abandoned and not been torched; if it was a professional nick, the car would have been taken to a safe workshop, repaired, and shipped abroad within hours rather than days. So the driver intended to murder Noyes . . ."

"I'll say it again, louder. Until Chambers is brought in and

153

questioned, the case is on full hold and you don't go within miles of Searle's place. Savvy?"

"It's a great life when you can wriggle out of trouble by whispering in the chief constable's ear."

"If you've only just understood that, it's small wonder that you've made a complete cock-up of everything."

Keen walked along to No. 27, rang the bell.

"Who is it?" Laura called out.

"Mike." The door opened and he stepped inside. "My contribution to the evening's pleasures," he said, as he handed her the plastic shopping bag.

She opened the bag and brought out the packet of smoked salmon.

"I hope you like it?"

"Yes, I do," she said flatly.

"You sound doubtful?"

"It's just . . . It was the special treat we sometimes gave ourselves."

"Then I should have found something else; some pâté." For how long was he going to keep tripping over Ralph's ghost?

"How were you to know?" She made an effort to be more cheerful. "I'll enjoy it. Go on through to the sitting room. Sandra's there."

"She's still up?"

"She wouldn't go to bed until she's said hullo to you."

A pity. As she crossed to the kitchen, he went into the sitting room. "How's Miss Ellis this evening?"

Sandra said scornfully: "Don't you know my name?"

"That is your name."

"It isn't."

"Then how's Sandra?" Bloody bad-tempered.

"She's nasty; she pulled my hair."

"Who did?"

"Merry. And I pulled her hair."

"Do you think that that made you a nasty girl as well?" he suggested, seizing the chance to deliver a sorely needed homily.

"I didn't cry, but I made her cry."

One wasted homily. "I called here yesterday evening, but the young lady who spoke to me through the front door wouldn't let me in. She said to go away or she'd call the police. That's amusing, isn't it?"

"Why?"

"I am a policeman."

"She's horrid. She tries to make me do things I don't want to do."

"That's good for the soul."

"I won't do anything she says."

"Does she often baby-sit when Mummy goes out?"

"I'm not a baby."

"Does she often keep you company?"

"She said she'd smack me if I kicked her again. I told Mummy that and so she won't be coming back."

Laura looked into the room. "Time to go up, love."

"No."

"It's long after your proper bedtime."

"I don't care."

"Isn't she impossible!" Laura said to Keen.

"No comment."

"Coward . . . Come on, Dra, be a good girl."

"I won't."

"I must get back to the kitchen . . . Mike, be a sweet and take Sandra up to bed, will you? I'll be a little time so perhaps you can read her a couple of pages."

"He doesn't read nice," Sandra said.

"Read nicely. And how can you know when he's never read to you? . . . There's the pinger so I must rush." She hurriedly left.

"Up to bed," he said.

"No."

155

"Would you like me to carry you?"

"I'll kick you."

"Then I won't carry you."

Sandra, a look of sullen defiance on her face, settled more firmly in the armchair. She struggled to stay awake, but soon was sprawled between the arms, fast asleep.

There was, he decided, very good reason to hope that when she was carried upstairs, she would not wake sufficiently to carry out her threat – she looked as if she had strong legs.

They ate on their laps. As Laura collected up the bowls in which they'd had apple pie and ice cream, she said: "Coffee?"

"If it's not too much trouble."

"How would you like it?"

"Black with a dash . . . Can I wash up while you're making the coffee?"

"No thanks. I never do it at night time. Switch the telly on if you like. It'll be the news soon." She left.

He decided not to watch the news and remain reasonably cheerful.

When she returned, she put a tray down on the low table, poured out two mugfuls of coffee. "Help yourself to milk and sugar."

He did so. "I called here last night." He sat back, mug in hand. "But I didn't go down very well. Whoever was inside threatened to call the police if I didn't leave."

She smiled briefly. "Lisa was recommended to me the other day, but she's not very intelligent and she threatened to smack Sandra for no reason, so she's not coming here again. She told me someone had called, but couldn't remember the name. It didn't occur to me it might have been you because we'd arranged for tonight."

"I felt at the bottom of the world and reckoned you'd help me climb up."

"Then I'm sorry I was out."

"Did you have a good evening?"

"Not really. I met an old friend whose husband also died suddenly last year. There were more tears than laughter."

Not out with a man!

When he kissed her goodnight, there was once again eagerness on his part, but little on hers. It was taking a long time to banish the ghost.

Sixteen

A ldridge threw the ball and Egan, his Jack Russell terrier, dashed after it with more zest than skill, then returned and waited impatiently to be told where it had gone.

"Over there," Aldridge pointed to his right at a large, tangled thicket. Egan began to hunt to his left. "You daft booger," he called out, his local accent thick. "When they was handing out brains, you was in another queue."

Egan rushed back and, head tilted, one ear folded back, eyes sparkling, mouth ajar, panting heavily, tail wagging, looked up at him.

"I reckon I'd have to pay to get someone to take you off me hands!" Money had been short since he'd lost his job and been compensated for many years' hard, loyal work by the minimum redundancy money, yet had he been offered thousands of pounds for Egan, he would have angrily rejected the offer.

The wood had been coppiced a few years back and the resulting space and light had spurred the undergrowth; it required considerable effort to force a way through it and in places the brambles had entwined to form thickets that were almost impenetrable. As far as he could judge, the ball had landed right in the centre of the one to his right. "Here, you can seek better than me. Go on."

Egan remained where he was and wagged his tail.

"Ain't you bred specially to face cover? The ball's in there, so bluddy well go on in and get it." He waved his hand, made encouraging noises, swore. He considered pushing Egan into

159

the thicket, quickly decided against the idea. A bramble thorn might rip the skin. A few months previously, a claw had ben split and the vet had had to cut it back and although a local anaesthetic had been used, Egan had screamed. He had felt as if the pain had been his as well as the dog's.

Should he leave the ball? Egan loved playing with it and must have one, but, like everything else, they cost so much more than he thought they should. He slowly walked around the thicket, visually searching for a patch of red, reached a point where displaced bramble vines and broken weed grass and willow-herb showed someone had recently forced a way into the centre of the thicket. He started along the trail, hoping he'd have a better chance of finding the ball. What he found was the torso of a man.

The pathologist, who had a regrettable sense of humour, said: "Apart from losing his head, I can't find any cause of death."

The detective superintendent managed a weak smile. "Is it OK to move him?"

"I've finished here." He stripped off surgical gloves and dropped them into a disposal bag, stepped out of his overalls, folded them up and placed them in another bag. "There are no distinguishing marks on the trunk, so until you find the head or arms, identification is going to be difficult."

Now tell me something I don't know, thought the detective superintendent, who was trying to conceal the nausea which had gripped him from the moment he'd approached the body. Twenty-two years of service had not inured him to some of the sights.

The pathologist left, walking between the marker stakes set out by the SOCOs.

The detective superintendent was grateful that he was not one of the men now searching every square inch of the surrounding land. The day was hot, the undergrowth hindered

all movement and, judging by the frequent swearing, the
brambles were studded with six-inch-long barbs.

The phone rang. Keen jerked awake and stared at the television screen for several seconds before he pulled himself
together and went out into the hall. As he approached the
telephone, it stopped ringing. Which perfectly summed up life.

He had not had any supper, so went through to the kitchen.
He searched in the store cupboard for a tin of baked beans,
finally remembered he'd opened the last one the previous day.
He had made a mental note to buy another when he shopped,
but had forgotten to shop. Two could not only live as cheaply
as one, they could live a damn sight better. He opened a tin of
sardines even though he didn't really like sardines. When life
was proving bloody, there could be perverse pleasure found in
making it even worse. He put two slices of bread in the toaster,
crossed to the refrigerator for butter and cheese. There was a
bag of radishes in the vegetable box. Radishes were a favourite
of Anne's. He threw them in the bin.

He was eating the last mouthful of toast and cheese when
the phone rang again. Showing more perversity, he did not
move. It continued to ring. He finally went through to the hall.

"I've been trying to get hold of you for hours," Fay said.

He pictured her – hair expensively fashioned, face expensively made up, body expensively clothed. When she walked
into a room, men began to fantasise. "Sorry."

"Is that all you can find to say? What a misery you can be!"

"It's my natural self surfacing."

"Or are you trying to make me think I ought to drive over
and cheer you up?"

He finally responded to her arch manner. "I'll have the
bedclothes turned back."

"What a conventional setting. Surely you can suggest something a little more interesting?"

"The toolshed?"

161

"God! Your humour's third-form. Which is why I love it. Mike, you know I don't like interfering in other people's lives . . ."

"Nothing gives you greater pleasure."

"Stop being a sod. You're coming here to dinner on Saturday."

"I am?"

"Tell me what your favourite meal is and I'll prepare it."

"Why? Have you fired the cook?"

"She's been inconsiderate enough to insist on having a holiday. She said she wanted to go to Rome for a day or two, so to persuade her to stay here, I warned her she'd probably get her bottom pinched all the time. That made the silly woman think she'd like to spend the whole fortnight there. What would you like to eat?"

"Roast swan."

"I don't think I'll be able to get that locally, but maybe my lovely little butcher in Soho will find me one."

"I doubt it. Most of them belong to the Queen."

"Then why say that's what you want? How annoying you can be! Just for that, you'll have to put up with bœuf en croûte because Ifor likes it. Be here at six."

"What about Anne?"

"She says she'll eat anything but boiled beef and carrots. I expect she was put off that dish by the awful song."

"I mean, will she be there on Saturday?"

"Of course she will."

"Then I don't think it's a good idea for me to come."

"Of course you don't because you're a stupid male with as much understanding of a woman's soul as a dead cod."

"If she knows I'm turning up, she'll take care to be somewhere else."

"When I say you're coming, she'll tell me I'm an interfering busybody and you're the last person she wants to meet. Then she'll ask if she can have a very little of the exquisite scent I've bought which costs so much that Ifor read me a lecture on extravagance until I reminded him of his new set of golf clubs."

"And you know why she'll want the scent?"

"To make herself irresistible."

"Because she knows I don't like women who douse themselves in smells."

"Moron! If I was within reach, I'd cripple your pride and joy for being so stupid. Now remember, you have to make her understand from your behaviour that you miss her more than you can bear and long for her return home. Cut out any stupid machismo. None of this being as much her fault as yours. You take all the blame. Meek submission."

"You're beginning to sound like an S-and-M dominatrix."

"I've never been clear about what fun and games they really get up to and when I ask Ifor, he professes not to know. I suspect the poor dear reckons that if he tells me, I'll start thinking he must have learned from experience. Six on Saturday, no argument. Understood?"

"If you say so."

"And don't forget, she loves freesias, so bring her the largest bunch you can find."

"When your house always looks like the Chelsea Flower Show?"

"God, you're a real primitive! A bunch of dandelions would say everything to her if you'd picked them – not that I suggest you do, for obvious sanitary reasons." She cut the connection.

He would have liked another drink, but common sense said to forgo it. He went through to the pantry and poured himself another.

At four thirty on Saturday afternoon, Keen was discussing the prospects, or the lack of them, of the English cricket team during the coming visit to Australia when Cain stepped into the room. "Mike, you're on surveillance."

"Sorry, Sarge, I'm on my way."

"That's right. To east Rainsham."

"I've a date I have to make."

"After the job's done, you can book yourself in with Madonna."

"It's vitally important . . ."

"So is this job. Hew's there now and you're to relieve him immediately. He'll give you all the gen."

If he'd explained why the dinner date was so important, it was probable Cain would have detailed someone else to do the job; his reluctance to admit the state of his marriage, however stupid that reluctance, stopped him from doing so.

Five and a half hours later, he drove the CID Fiesta into the car park at divisional HQ, climbed out and crossed to his Astra. As he opened the driving door, there was a call.

He turned. Two PCs, now in civvies, came across.

"Just finished our turn," Cannon said, "and going along to the Duke's Head to wash out the taste. Are you with us?"

Since the evening as planned had turned out to be a total frost, why not?

He was awoken by ringing. He would have taken the phone and thrown it through the window if he'd had that much energy. During the night, someone had emptied the contents of a dustbin into his mouth, someone else was now trying to fracture his skull with a seven-pound hammer, and his stomach was in a state of revolution. He reached out to the phone on the bedside table. "Yes?" he croaked.

"As I thought!"

That was all he needed. Anne at her coldest.

"You were so damned rude last night because you were boozing and had forgotten you'd been invited to dinner."

"If you want to know the truth . . ."

"There's no point in listening to you."

He tried to speak reasonably. "I was getting ready to leave

the station to come back here to shower and change before driving over to you when I got sent off on a surveillance job."

"And it was beyond your ability to phone Fay and explain?"

"There was a chance I'd still be able to get away in time, so I left it. Then, doing the surveillance, I couldn't break off to find a phone."

"When did you finish?"

"Well after ten," he answered, adding time.

"What stopped you ringing then to say what had happened?"

"I reckoned it was too late."

"You're trying to persuade me you thought Fay and Ifor would be in bed and asleep before midnight at the earliest? You know as well as I do that they're night owls. I suppose it still hasn't begun to occur to you that Fay went to a lot of trouble for you?"

"Of course it has."

"But that's no reason to bother yourself to the extent of ringing up and apologising? Other people simply don't matter."

"When the job was finished, I was worn out . . ."

"Too worn out to ring and apologise? Apologies don't come easily, do they, because you see them as a sign of weakness. The macho man just stamps through life, not giving a damn who he treads on or kicks out of the way."

"You've no right to say that."

"That's a laugh, coming from someone who makes an Essex yobbo look like a cultivated gentleman."

With a flash of inspiration, he remembered the freesias he'd bought the previous day. "Would it interest you to hear I've been out and bought some flowers and I'm going to drive over later on and give them to her as a humble apology?"

After a moment, she said: "You've bought flowers on a Sunday?"

He struggled to clear his scrambled mind. "The garden centre on the main road is open today."

"Bit of a risky drive, surely? Judging by how you sound, if

you'd been stopped in the car by one of your comrades, you'd still have been ripe enough to send the breathalyser off the scale."

Her mood seemed to have softened slightly. "In the search for forgiveness, no risk is too great."

"It's no good your driving over here later on, Mike."

"Why not?"

"Ifor's promised to take Judy to the new theme park for children and we three adults are declaring ourselves young for the day."

"I'll leave the flowers by the back door with a note to Fay." A note to plead that she did not disclose she had suggested buying the freesias the previous day for Anne. "Maybe you'll accept then that I'm not lying."

"I didn't say you were."

"Your tone did."

"Just as yours tells me right now that you'd shy away from a plateful of eggs and bacon."

How right she was! "Is Judy better?"

"Virtually back to normal."

"I miss you both and want to be with you."

"Which you would have done had you come to dinner yesterday."

Her mood had not softened. "Can't you appreciate how things were for me? I'd been looking forward to an evening with you, but had to spend it in the back of a van which smelled as if it had been carting corpses around. And just to cap everything, the operation turned out to be a complete dud. It made me so frustrated that when Hal suggested a drink . . . Well, I went along."

"You need to find someone who doesn't mind that you're always thinking of number one because half the time you forget that there's a number two."

Right now, number one felt even worse than he had before.

Seventeen

I nglebrant divisional HQ phoned on the second of June, a day of sun, light breeze, and puffball clouds.

"We searched the wood on hands and knees and found booger all."

The story of police work, Cain thought as he started to draw a circle on the sheet of paper in front of himself.

"So all we had was a torso with no bits and pieces to say who he was. The Guv'nor's had us checking dustbins, rubbish collection points, landfills . . . What did we find? Booger all."

The circle became a ragged oval. Some time ago, he'd read that no one, not even the finest artist, could draw a perfect circle freehand and since then he'd been trying to prove that wrong. Constant failure was leading him to think it might be right.

"But the lab boys have just come up trumps. They took a sample and worked out the DNA and that's been compared with the DNA database of convicted criminals. Up has come Edward Chambers's name."

Cain forgot circles.

"And seeing as you lot's been asking for information, I thought I'd get straight onto you."

"Can you say anything more?"

"Not as yet. The lads are out, asking questions, but I'd be surprised if they learn anything useful. When a bloke gets his head and limbs hacked off, people's memories slip."

Cain thanked the other, agreed that both life and work were

becoming more of a booger every day, rang off. He left his room and went along to the DI's. Drew was not there. He wrote a brief note.

Drew, who'd been pacing behind his desk, came to a halt. "Once again, there's no certainty."

"He is dead," Keen said.

Drew ignored that. "It's never been more than supposition Chambers was driving the car which ran down Noyes. He boasted he'd done a good job down south, but south of where?" He sat, rubbed his chin, tapped on the desk with his fingers. "That list you had drawn up of jobs carried out during the relevant period which might have used a top wheel was nearly as long as my arm. He might have been on any of those rather than running down Noyes."

"But were any of them so sensitive that the moment he started spending and boasting, he had to be rubbed out?"

"When someone's mouth becomes too slack, one man will have him taken out, another won't, irrespective of what's at stake."

"His death fits in."

"Only if one can be certain Noyes was murdered and not killed by criminally careless driving."

"But—"

"I do know all the arguments. Where do we go from here?"

Cain said nothing; he had long ago learned that ideas were best left to others.

"No suggestions?"

"One, sir," Keen said. "If we prove the money in the deed box demonstrably has to be from blackmail, paid by Searle, we'd be able to join things up."

"How do we do that?"

"Examine Searle's bank accounts for large withdrawals in cash."

"First, the hard evidence in hand does not warrant applying

for the authority to do that; secondly, without proof of the dates when Noyes received payments in cash, there can be no meaningful connection."

"There may just be a way."

"Which is?"

"Noyes was a small-minded man with a vindictive character. He told Miss Logan that he went on cruises to make a nuisance of himself and get his own back. It's difficult to make any sense of that unless one accepts that when he served at sea as a steward he frequently suffered rudeness from passengers who had the money, but not the manners to know how to behave. He, in turn, and when he could afford it, went cruising, probably to act as objectionably as possible towards the crew. Along the same lines, when he returned from a cruise, he made a point of telling Miss Logan how luxurious and expensive it had been, hoping to arouse her jealousy and resentment because in the old days, when she'd been young, she'd have looked down on his type and now he was looking down on her."

"Balls!" Cain exclaimed.

"Carry on," Drew said.

"If I'm right, he'll have gone cruising as soon as possible after Searle paid blackmail money. So if we can match at least some withdrawals with cruises, there's proof."

"I'd hardly call that proof."

"This is a case of circumstantial evidence and so up to a point it can't be strong enough to take to court; but if and when that point's reached, the coincidences, the possibilities, the probabilities, the presumptions become too many and fit too closely to leave room for doubt. Show an obvious connection between the cash withdrawals and the cruises and then surely we're at that point?"

Drew stood, began to pace the floor once more. "We're in something of a catch twenty-two situation. We can't obtain the evidence that might make a case until we get a sighting of

Searle's bank statements; we can't apply for the authority to examine those until we can claim we have sufficient proof to provide justification."

"Then say we do have the proof."

"On the grounds that the means justify the end? I suppose if the dates do match up, it could be successfully argued that there had been proof enough since in retrospect the evidence we now have will be strengthened. But it's a gamble."

"A gamble which can't fail."

Drew stopped pacing.

There was a long silence.

"It would be amusing to see the great Cedric Searle in the dock," he said.

"Small reason to risk . . ." Cain began.

"Quite," he snapped angrily.

Keen made little of what had just been said until he remembered the friend of Drew's who had been dismissed from the force when Searle was chairman of the Police Authority.

Drew sat. "Any request for authority to examine Searle's bank accounts requires my signature. I am not prepared to give it even though if the search produces a negative result he should be unaware the request was made since the banks accept that whenever possible it is to everyone's advantage for silence unless and until a charge is brought. However, it is my firm judgement that at the moment there is insufficient weight of evidence to warrant the request and since the rules forbid my gambling on possibilities, that has to be that." He stared into space. "Brings to mind a case I had when a DC. I needed the Guv'nor's signature, but he wasn't around and the case was obviously going to go down the tubes unless something could be done immediately. So I took the risk, as one does when young, of claiming his authority to sign on his behalf. Luckily, things worked out as hoped and although my forgery was uncovered by him, all I suffered was a bollocking for form's sake; after that was over, he took me out for a drink.

Six months later, the case provided a commendation on his flimsy."

"The end justified the means," Keen said.

"We live in a time when moral values have all but vanished, consequently there is little that is not justified by success . . . I'll agree that your reading of events may very well be correct, but unless the investigation into Chambers's murder can show a connection with Noyes's death and thereby provide a peg to hang all the circumstantial evidence on, this case is in the deep freeze . . . Right, that's it."

Keen and Cain left. Cain turned into his room, Keen hesitated, then followed him. Cain settled behind the desk, began to roll a cigarette.

"Did you get the same impression I did?" Keen asked.

"Being someone who keeps both feet on the ground, I doubt it."

"I think the Guv'nor was saying that in his present position he has to play things by the book, but an application for permission to examine Searle's bank accounts should be put through by someone."

Cain licked the gummed edges of the paper, pulled loose a small trail of tobacco and replaced this in the pouch. "If you'd as much common sense as a half-witted coot, you'd stop up your ears to what you've been thinking."

Keen settled on the settee, but did not use the remote control to activate the television. Cain had made his opinion very clear – justice came a poor second to self-preservation. But he was motivated by the fear that if anything went wrong, he would be caught up in the fallout. Drew had made his position very much less clear, yet it surely had been unmistakable? Since they now seemed to be offered a good chance of finding the necessary proof, that chance should be seized, even if it meant unorthodox action on someone's part. However disillusioned a policeman became after years of seeing his work negated by

171

bureaucratic stupidity, legal niceties, and political incompetence, if he were true to his job, justice remained his goal.

He suddenly questioned whether his memories of Berenice Searle's autocratic attitude and Drew's memories of the dismissal from the force of his friend could be playing any part in their desire to see the case broken wide open? He switched on the television.

Eighteen

F ew inhabitants of Michenhall knew the name could be traced back to Mixenhall and those who did remained silent; who willingly explained that he lived in a place whose origins appeared to have been a dung heap?

Despite its name, it was a typical coastal town. The large buildings along the front had been hotels before the advent of mass foreign travel and were now converted into flats; many of the shops sold the kind of mementoes that were thrown away by the donee as soon as the donor was out of sight; none of the restaurants would enjoy even a footnote in any food guide; the bungalows and small houses which stretched back for nearly a mile were frequently inhabited by retired people who had come south for a warmer and more comfortable life and soon regretted the move.

The curving beach of sand was still promoted as the Golden Crescent of the South. On the Sunday, an off-duty day, Keen drove Laura and Sandra to the beach for a picnic, English style – pretending the clouds weren't there and it was so warm the breeze was welcome.

"You do like tomato sandwiches, don't you?" Laura asked.

"My favourite."

They both laughed.

Sandra was digging in the sand with the wooden spade he'd bought her. She'd actually thanked him. What's more, earlier she had seemed quite glad to see him again. Thanks to his tact and patience, their relationship was moving into smoother waters. Which must make Laura happier ... He turned to look at her. She had drawn up her skirt above her knees and the wind was catching the hem and billowing it so that at irregular intervals much of her thigh was visible. Her skin looked very smooth to the touch.

"A penny for them," she said suddenly.

"It'll cost you far more than that."

"No deal. I can guess."

She probably could. Laura had spoken in a coquettish manner. A good sign. Perhaps circumstances were melding to bring the future nearer than he had judged likely ...

Sandra came running across the sand and stopped in front of them. "I want to go swimming."

"We haven't brought your costume and anyway, it's not warm enough," Laura said.

"Lots of people are swimming."

"I can't see anyone in the water."

"They've just got out ... I want to swim." She gripped Laura's arm and began to shake it.

"Please stop doing that, Dra."

"I won't until you say I can."

"You're hurting me."

"I want to go swimming." Sandra tightened her grip.

Laura gave a quick gasp of pain.

Keen reached across and gripped Sandra's wrist, forced her to let go of her mother's arm. She stared at him for several seconds, then began to cry.

"What are you doing?" Laura's voice was high.

"Making certain you aren't hurt any more," he answered.

"He's broken my arm!" Sandra blubbered.

"Oh, my God!" Laura exclaimed.

"Which arm have I broken?" he asked. "Show me."

Sandra raised her right one.

"If it were really broken, you wouldn't be able to lift it."

174

She considered that for a while. "I hate you," she finally announced.

"Then you won't want to come with me to that shop and find out if their ice cream is really as good as the notice says, will you?"

"When?"

"After we've eaten."

She picked up her spade and ran to the water's edge where she began to dig a channel.

"You shouldn't have done that," Laura said.

"She was hurting you."

"Not really."

"Then why did you cry out?"

She avoided the question. "You tricked her by asking her to raise her arm. That was unfair."

"One has to be unfair where children are concerned in order to be on level terms. And it always strikes me as a good idea to make a child realise for herself that her lie's not being believed."

"She wasn't lying. She imagines things."

"I'd say that in this instance, the distinction's a bit fine."

"She's my daughter and I don't want you doing anything like that again."

Was it only a short while ago that he'd been congratulating himself that he was getting on so well with Sandra that Laura must smile at him? He apologised for what he had done and his apology was graciously accepted with not too many reservations.

Laura came downstairs and into the sitting room. "She's asleep, at last."

"When one's young, one doesn't want to go to bed; when one's older, one can't get to bed quickly enough."

"Speak for yourself."

She was smiling. He'd made up the lost ground.

"Would you like to pour yourself another drink?"

"That's a proposition to which there can be only one answer. What about you?"

"Maybe just a small one."

He poured out two gins and tonic of equal size. Before going upstairs, she had been sitting on an armchair, now she was on the settee. He handed her a glass, sat down by her side. He raised his glass. "To us."

"I'm sorry I went for you this morning," she said.

"It's a mother's privilege."

"It always upsets me so when Sandra cries."

"Of course. But I'll bet she does that whenever she's not getting her own way."

"I don't suppose you can understand . . ." She became silent.

"That you find it very difficult to deny her anything because she's all you're left with?"

"I . . . Maybe."

"Don't take too much offence when I say that in the long run it'll be better for Sandra if you show her there are times when tears won't get her what she wants."

"I suppose you're right . . . No, I know you're right. But it's so difficult for me to say no."

"Then I'll stop complaining."

"And that's a typically male comment!"

He put his arm along the back of the settee and rested his fingertips on her neck. She did not move.

"Really, you're very patient with her," she said.

Len claimed that the surest way into a woman's bed was to praise her child. "She's a charming girl who's facing up to things far better than most could or would."

"She didn't mean it when she said she hates you."

"I hardly took it seriously."

She snuggled up against him.

"How about another day on the beach?" he asked.

176

"Please."

"Maybe next time it will be warm enough for Sandra to go into the water. Can she swim?"

"Not really."

"Perhaps I could try to teach her?"

"That would be wonderful."

"The sooner a youngster's taught, the better. There's a girl in the States who started learning when she was one and at the age of fourteen recently swam the length of Lake Superior."

"When it's three hundred and eighty-three miles long?"

"Are you sure it is?"

"That's one of the few facts from school geography I remember. And I can't think why I do."

"Obviously to shoot me down in flames. Maybe it was that she swam part of the length of Lake Superior."

"Just maybe!" She laughed. Her lips were close to his.

He kissed her. After the briefest hesitation, she relaxed and allowed his tongue to explore. He raised his right arm and cupped her left breast through the light cotton dress, gently stroked with his thumb the point where he estimated the nipple must lie under a brassière that was too secure to allow certainty.

He removed his right hand, brought his left arm round and down and inside her frock. His fingers reached the edge of the brassière, but could not slip easily under it; he pulled the left cup up and over her breast. He fondled the nipple and she began to make the sound at the back of her throat that had a man's mind filled with shooting stars. He slid his right hand over her knee and under her skirt. She parted her legs . . .

"Mummy, Mummy," came a shout from upstairs.

She pulled his right hand free, somehow wriggled his left hand out of her dress, stood and hurried out of the room, straightening her clothes as she went.

He was frustrated, but not wholly surprised when, on returning downstairs, she carefully sat in one of the armchairs. When momentum was lost, so was all future progress.

177

"She suddenly woke up and wanted to know I was all right. That's rather sweet, isn't it?" Laura said.

He would have given a different description.

Metcalfe had removed his jacket and sat behind the desk in his braces. There was a touch of the bookmaker about him. "The last time you were here, I expressed surprise you should have questioned Mr Searle several times because of what was no more than a wild theory." His manner did not possess its usual bluffness; it was openly antagonistic.

Drew had been left to stand.

"And I said the matter was not to be taken any further until there was hard evidence to warrant such action. Yet we have received a very strong complaint from London solicitors which challenges our latest action and threatens grave legal consequences. The CC is tearing his hair out."

Somewhat difficult, since he was virtually bald, Drew irrationally thought.

"I explained to the CC that I had given orders for no further action to be taken. He has told me to identify the person responsible for disregarding my orders." Metcalfe leaned forward until his stomach pressed against the edge of the desk. "And that's precisely what I intend to bloody well do."

"Sir, as far as I know, Mr Searle has not been questioned again . . ."

"Don't start trying to feed me crap. You know what I'm talking about."

"On the contrary."

"You're trying to tell me you've no idea what's got the solicitors shouting?"

"That's right."

"Then I'll tell you. You gave authority for a D One Six application. When Searle discovered one of his banks had been asked for details of any accounts of his they held, he went straight to his solicitors."

"How did he learn what was happening?"

"How the devil do you think? The bank told him."

"They're supposed to keep quiet about any application."

"That's convention, nothing more. Officially, their duty is to their client unless they are legally relieved of that duty."

"Why break the convention this time?"

"Because Mr Searle is not Mr Smith. You really thought a bank would keep its mouth shut where a man in his position is concerned? He walks along different paths."

Drew could see his career disappearing down the plughole. "Sir, I did not sign a D One Six request naming Mr Searle."

Metcalfe leaned back in his chair, rested his thumbs under his braces. "The solicitors say it's in your name."

"I repeat, I did not sign it. Nor did I authorise its being sent."

"Then who the hell did?"

"I can't say for the moment, but I have a rough idea."

"The DC with an imagination that runs bloody riot?"

"He seems to be the most likely possibility."

"Find out if it was him – if so, he's on suspension right away . . . And mark this. I expect my DIs to know what's going on in their manors, not have to hear about it from me."

Drew said nothing.

"I want to learn bloody fast that it's been sorted out. Understand?"

He left.

Keen entered the DI's office and came to a halt in front of the desk. "You wanted to speak to me, sir?"

"Shut the door."

He shut the door.

"I am just back from the ACC. He told me Searle's solicitors are threatening legal action because banks have been given D One Six notices which name him. Are you responsible for those notices?"

"Yes, sir."

"Why?"

"It seemed the bank accounts offered us the only way of making a breakthrough in this case."

"Who signed the notices?"

"I did." ˙

"In whose name?"

"In yours, sir."

"You are admitting you forged my signature?"

"Hardly. It was done at your suggestion."

"I made no such suggestion."

"Not directly, maybe. But you carefully told us about when you were a DC and you signed in your DI's name to ensure a case went through."

"I made it very clear that I did that with his full knowledge and therefore had his authority."

"No, sir. You said you did it off your own bat. But because the case worked out, when the DI discovered you'd signed his name all he did was deliver an official reprimand and then take you out for a drink."

"I have no time for officers who try to lie to me."

"I am merely repeating what you said to the sarge and me."

"I made it absolutely clear that at the time I had the DI's say-so to sign in his name."

"Then why should he reprimand you?"

"The rules required it since they did not grant specific authority for unorthodox action whatever the circumstances."

"When I said that what had happened proved the means had justified the end, you remarked they always did in a world where only success counted. That suggests—"

"It suggests you are trying every means you can think of to escape responsibility for an action that negates the entire ethos of our work. On the ACC's orders, you are suspended from duty as of now."

"Preusmably you lied to him?"

"Insolence hardly helps you."

"It's insolence to defend myself? I'm supposed to be supine and let you walk all over me? . . . You're teaching me that I'm still wet behind the ears. When you told me how you'd forged the DI's signature, I reckoned that in a roundabout way you were saying to put the request through in your name; it didn't occur to me that you were making certain you could reap the rewards if we struck lucky, but were covering yourself if anything went wrong."

"A senior officer from County will confirm your suspension as soon as possible. I want your warrant card."

Keen brought from his pocket the small black plastic wallet which contained the card and threw it on the desk. "And I imagined we were a team!"

He left, found Cain was not in his office, continued on to the CID general room. Only Soper was present. "Have you seen the sarge?" he asked.

"Not recently . . . You sound like something's just made your day. Had your car clamped?"

"I've been suspended from duty."

"Jeez, man, what gives? Someone caught you and the little blonde in the computer room playing too many games?"

"I made the mistake of trusting the Guv'nor."

"Didn't anyone ever tell you, never trust a senior since he carries the clout? I hope it's not too serious?"

Did Soper imagine he'd been suspended for spitting to windward?

"Say, have I told you about the little number I met at the end of last week who thought playing it cool meant stripping off before beginning? When she . . ."

Keen ceased to listen. Soper liked to think of himself as Don Juan's successor, but his present boasting was a way of diverting the conversation; he was not the man to risk sympathising with another's misfortunes.

181

Nineteen

K een had been home for no more than ten minutes when
the phone rang.

"Daddy, I kept calling and calling yesterday, but you
weren't there," Judy said in a rush of words. "Then Aunty
Fay told me to try to talk to you at work, but they said you
weren't there also."

"I'm sorry I wasn't around."

"You are to have lunch with me."

"Nothing would be more fun. Where shall we go?"

"It's a secret for Aunty Fay and me."

"I'm terribly sorry and it's very stupid of me, but I'm not
quite understanding you."

"Because you won't listen. Mummy's going to Astonford to
look at a flat, or something, because she says we can't go on
living here. But I like it and Aunty Fay says I can stay as long
as I like. Why don't you come and live here?"

"Hasn't Mummy explained?"

"Uncle Ifor says he'll give me riding lessons for my birthday. Isn't that super?"

"Wonderful. But try not to fall off the horse and land on
your head."

"You are silly! Of course I won't . . . Here's Aunty Fay."

After a brief pause, Fay said: "How's my second favourite
boyfriend?"

"Wondering who your first is."

"What if I tell you?"

183

"I'll charge him with something to get him out of the way."

"Wonderful caveman stuff . . . Is Sunday all right?"

"Why ask me?"

"For Heaven's sake, Mike, swallow your pride."

"I'll swallow most things if I know what I'm putting in my mouth."

"Judy's just told you."

"She confused me to the point where it seems we are to have a secret meal together and neither of us is to know when or where."

"I just don't believe you're confused. My mother always said that when a man's determined to be difficult, the only solution is to give him what he most wants because then he'll be reasonable for a little while."

"I'll be with you in minutes to claim my desire."

"I won't be here. I'm taking Judy out to buy her a frock and if we don't leave soon she'll become so impatient she'll probably drive the car herself. I don't think the insurance will cover her and Ifor's so fussy about that sort of thing. So tell me quickly, when it will be most convenient to come to lunch?"

"Are you serious? You're asking me after last week's fiasco?"

"As I said to Anne, boys will be boys."

"And what was her reaction to that?"

"To wonder if you'd ever grow up sufficiently to be a boy . . . The party's a secret between Judy and me and I've promised her a large box of special chocolates if she keeps quiet about it. I'll tell Ifor to open a bottle of Bollinger and I'll make certain Anne has at least one glassful before you arrive so that she's in a good mood."

"Which will dissipate the moment I arrive."

"When you talk like that, I want to empty a bowl of custard over your head. Remember, no boozing, no forgetting, and most of all, no chasing after whoever it was caught your fancy yesterday."

"No one did."

"Because I adore you, you can tell me you weren't at home
or at work because you were running a marathon and I'll
believe you. But remember that Anne's worth a dozen of
whoever she is. Now, when can you manage?"

"Whatever day suits you best."

"A man of leisure?"

"More or less."

"No wonder crime in the country is a flourishing product.
Let's make it Thursday, then. Write that down in your diary
and underline it three times. And I'll ring you in the morning
to remind you that it's no blondes for the day. You do realise,
don't you, that a woman who'll fake the colour of her hair will
fake something else that a man thinks so important? Now
listen very carefully. Your lovely wife is unhappy and beginning to blame herself as well as you for all that's happened, not
least because you had the grace to bring me some lovely
freesias as an apology."

"I hope you didn't let on . . ."

"Don't be so insulting. Of course I didn't tell her they were
really meant for her. So because she's blaming herself, I'm
losing no opportunity to agree with her that it is both your
faults – keep the conscience stirred is the motto of the day. So
when you turn up, she'll want to say how sorry she is, but pride
will try to keep her mute. That means it's up to you to
manoeuvre her into a quiet corner where you tell her that
really and truly it's all your fault, you're a real bastard to cause
her so much distress, and without her life is a black hole. Her
conscience will be digging so hard that she'll burst into tears
and ask if you can ever forgive her."

"To the accompaniment of a Hollywood choir?"

"Just shut up! Like every true hero, you again take all the
blame and assure her that you've nothing to forgive and as you
hold her to your bosom you promise to fight dragons for her.
We women are suckers for a little romantic chivalry. Now you

185

can have your choir. Singing that lovely song from *Kismet* about holding hands and paradise. Is that all understood?"

"Understood. Fay . . ."

"What?"

"I don't know how to thank you for everything, but on Thursday I'll get you into another quiet corner and try."

"Try what?"

"To make you understand how I feel."

"Tactile explanations can be rather overexciting." She laughed before she said goodbye and rang off.

He went into the sitting room. Fay was frothy, but no fool. So Anne was blaming herself as well as him for the break-up. Reconciliation was possible. The world was suddenly becoming golden . . . It returned to brass. He was on suspension. Suspension would almost certainly turn into dismissal. No job, no pension. Would even a contrite Anne want to return to that kind of a future?

When Keen walked into the front room at divisional HQ, the duty PC's, "Morning, Mike," was spoken in a tone that made it clear he knew about the suspension, but did not reveal whether his reaction to this was curiosity, sympathy, or a desire to steer well clear. Keen made his way up to the fifth floor and the detective sergeant's room.

"Didn't expect to see you," was Cain's surly greeting.

"I want a word."

"The matter's way out of my hands."

Keen moved a chair and sat. Cain, noticeably uneasy, began to roll a cigarette.

"Has the Guv'nor told you he informed the ACC he'd specifically said the banks weren't to be approached?"

Cain finished rolling the cigarette.

"And that I signed the application form in his name without his authority?"

"Well?"

186

"He agreed with me that the details of Searle's bank accounts might provide the evidence we needed."

Cain struck a match. "But he judged there was insufficient hard evidence to warrant an application."

"Sure. But then went on to tell us about the time he was a DC and took the risk of signing in his DI's name."

"Senior officers often waste time boring the likes of us with their reminiscences."

"He was encouraging me to bend the rules and sign the application form in his name. You know that as well as me."

"I know nothing of the sort."

"You thought the same or you wouldn't have said what you did afterwards."

"What did I say?"

"That if I'd any sense, I'd forget what I was thinking. You accepted he'd been encouraging me. But now he's doing his damnedest to evade any responsibility."

"What d'you expect?"

"That he accepts the consequences of what he said."

"When that would scupper his chances of climbing any higher up the promotion ladder and might well even slip him down a rung?"

"He kicks me into the shit so that he can stay out of it?"

"Now you're beginning to understand."

"He's out of luck. When I'm hauled up before the internal inquiry, I'll tell them he actively encouraged me to sign the application in his name."

"He'll deny that."

"My word's better than his."

"You can't be that stupid."

"My word will be corroborated."

"How?"

"By you."

The cigarette had gone out. Cain relit it.

"We're a team. I always thought the DI was in it, but he's

made it very clear that he looks after number one and doesn't give a toss about anyone else. Maybe all senior officers are like that when it comes to the bottom line. But the rest of us aren't. So I know that when the hearing asks what really was said when we were with the DI, you'll tell them."

Cain stubbed out the cigarette. "I'll tell them I heard the DI say that no action was to be taken."

After a while, Keen said: "You as well?"

Cain stared down at the ashtray.

"Too scared of authority to speak the truth? Too scared to remember you're supposed to be part of the team? I've obviously been walking around with my eyes shut."

Cain looked up and at the far wall. "You've been walking around with your head in the clouds."

"Because I thought there was such a thing as loyalty?"

"Talk's easy when you're young. But when you're my age and there's a family to keep, one of whom has left home but got herself into so much financial pain she still has to be helped, you need a job and a pension more than most anything else."

"They can't strip away your pension rights because you tell the truth."

"You think I'd survive if I put the feelers on my own DI?" He began to roll another cigarette. "I tried to warn you, but you wouldn't listen."

"So it's all my fault?"

"Call it the system's fault if that'll make you feel any better."

It didn't.

Twenty

K een went through to the hall and picked up the receiver.
"It's Laura. I wondered if you're all right?"

"I'm fine."

"That's good. It's just that . . . I thought you'd be along before now."

"I've been up to my neck with work."

"It wasn't because I . . ."

"You what?"

"Nothing. I want you to know you've made me realise I've been letting Sandra have her own way much too often. She's needed discipline, as all children do, and I've not understood that."

Had she been rereading the later works of Dr Spock? "I'm no longer an ogre?"

"You were never that . . . Are you sure everything's all right? You don't sound as if . . . well . . ."

His father had been something of a Puritan and fond of saying that one reaped as one sowed. He'd turned to Laura because Anne had rejected him, now Anne was ready to receive him back. That made Laura . . . He stifled his conscience before it could provide an answer. "If I sound spaced out it's because I'm so tired from work that I'm liable to fall asleep between words."

"Then you won't want to go on talking to me." She paused, then continued in a voice which did not completely mask her disappointment. "I just wanted to make certain nothing was wrong."

"For which, many thanks."

"We'll see you again soon?"

"Of course."

"Then sleep well and long."

As he replaced the receiver, he wondered how he was going to be able to cause her the least possible emotional pain when he told her that Anne was returning to him?

He went through to the larder and poured himself a generous drink. Human relationships, good or bad, could tie a man into a granny knot.

Wednesday gave summer a bad name. The sky was heavily overcast with dirty grey clouds and the easterly wind was chilly; the sun might have departed to another galaxy.

Keen left his car in the council car park and walked briskly from there to the jewellers. As he entered the shop, the door "pinged" and Culrose looked out from the small room beyond. He came forward to stand behind the glass-topped counter in which were several digital watches, a line he disliked but stocked – time should be captured by workmanship, not electronics. "Good morning. Are you bringing me another of Pierce's confections?"

Keen had to search his memory to identify Pierce as the maker of Searle's signet ring. "It's a personal visit this time. I'm looking for something to give Anne to mark a celebration."

"Then, as I mentioned the last time we spoke, I have a sapphire ring which will compliment her almost as much as she will complement it."

Had someone younger in age as well as speech said that, it would have sounded pedantically stupid; from Culrose, however, it was the compliment intended. "Something – in other words, my salary – tells me it's way beyond my range."

"I would make you a special offer."

"I'm afraid my maximum is a hundred pounds."

190

"How often facts defeat wishes! . . . Are you looking for a piece of jewellery?"

"Not necessarily."

"Good. On a plain woman, a piece of gimcrack jewellery is unbecoming; on a beautiful woman, such as Anne, it is an insult. So do you have a suggestion?"

"I've come here for you to provide that."

"Then how about a silver brooch? Silver is sadly under-rated, yet not only is it most attractive, when worked with taste it is excellent value. Is Anne fond of animals?"

"Just so long as they don't have eight legs."

"She likes dogs?"

"Her family always had Lakeland terriers and she brought hers with her when we married. But after Judy was born, Tyke became so jealous of her that we had to have him put down. Anne was so upset by this that it's only recently she's begun to talk about one day having another."

"A Lakeland . . . Let us see what we have." Culrose turned and took three steps to a cabinet, which he unlocked. He brought out a tray, lined with blue velvet, in which were several small silver brooches featuring dogs. He placed the tray on the counter in front of Keen. "These are made in Italy, a country which still possesses an artistic soul." He bent closer to the tray. "I think fortune smiles on us." He picked up a brooch, read the label attached to it. "Fortune proves to be as fickle as ever. An Airedale." He replaced it, visually examined the other brooches. He straightened up. "Most regrettably, no Lakeland terrier."

"Can I have a look at the Airedale?"

He passed it across. "I venture to suggest that this is so beautifully sculpted that when one looks at it, one has the impression that even the individual hairs are there. True art. A really great painting is one that makes the viewer see so much more than is actually depicted; for a brief moment, he is granted the same depth of vision that the painter had."

191

Keen studied the dog – head cocked, tail proud, a happy-go-lucky terrier. "Would you know that that wasn't a Lakeland?"

"As you must have gathered, I was certain that it was one before I read the label. My mistake is, of course, no reflection on the artist. Apart from size, the appearance of the two breeds is very similar; very similar indeed."

"If I remove the label and say it's a Lakeland, she's not going to doubt that, is she?"

"I'm sure it will be a secret which you and I alone will share," Culrose said with conspiratorial pleasure.

"How much is it?"

"What will you say if I quote you sixty-five pounds?"

"Thanks very much and do you take cheques?"

"When it is yours, I do not even ask to see a guarantee card."

Five minutes later, Keen left the shop. As he walked back to the car park, he visualised Anne's excitement – she enjoyed receiving almost as much as giving – as she unwrapped the little presentation box and lifted the lid to see the silver Tyke. She would perhaps shed a tear for the past, then suggest they buy a puppy. And Judy would dance as she detailed all the things she and the puppy would do together . . .

Thursday restored summer. The sky was cloudless, the sunshine warm, the breeze light. The gods were with him, Keen decided, as he fried a second egg as a celebration.

Time, according to experts, was relative which explained why, when he'd finished eating breakfast, it began to crawl until every minute became five; but eventually it was half-past eleven. He made certain for the umpteenth time that the small, gift-wrapped jewel box was in his pocket, then left the house. As he walked the hundred yards to where his car was parked, he heard an engine start up and rev fiercely, but took no notice of that. He reached the Astra and stepped out onto the road, began to go around the bonnet to the driving door. He heard a squeal of tyres, but once again did not consciously place any significance in the fact. He brought the car key out of his trouser pocket . . .

Abruptly, he was seized with so overwhelming a certainty that he had to get out of the way that against all the canons of logical behaviour he spun round and began to race back to the pavement. There was the hideous screech of metal against metal, then a glancing blow to his side flung him forward and into the car ahead. He struggled to identify the departing car. Black. A Mercedes? Registration letters OF or OE . . . Letters and numbers dissolved into a blur as pain ripped through his body, then he lost consciousness.

Twenty-One

R egaining consciousness was a bewildering, painful, frustrating experience.

"Hi! I'm Linda."

The last thing he wanted was social introductions while fire roamed around his body.

"You'll be very glad to hear that although the bruising is severe, nothing's broken. You're lucky."

Given the chance, he'd let her experience his pain for a few seconds, so she could understand just how lucky he felt. He opened his eyes and stared up at a nurse whose features suggested home cooking rather than Marilyn Monroe.

"How are you feeling?"

Bloody awful. But for some peculiar reason, an Englishman was expected to keep the upper lip at attention. "Not so bad," he mumbled.

"Dr Hesketh will soon be along to examine you." She moved away.

He looked to his right. The man in the next bed said hullo and how was he feeling; he looked to his left and the man in the next bed said hullo and how was he feeling? He closed his eyes and remembered he'd read that in order to escape pain, all one needed to do was imagine there was none. He imagined, but pain proved stronger than his imagination.

Dr Hesketh – tall, thin, chillingly precise – said he'd escaped serious injury and did he have full movement in the digits of his right hand? He waggled all four fingers and thumb. "Good," Dr Hesketh said. "You're a lucky man." He would have enjoyed raising two fingers to that.

He slept. When he awoke, it occurred to him to phone the station and tell them an attempt had been made to murder him which confirmed everything he'd maintained from the beginning of the Searle case. He called out to a passing nurse and explained he needed a telephone.

If he wanted to inform a relative of his situation, she would give his message to the office and they would make the call, otherwise he would have to wait until he could make his way down to the public phones in reception.

After the nurse had left, the man in the bed to his right, said: "You want to make a call, mate?"

"Yes, and it's important. Why can't they bring a phone along and plug it in?"

"That's what I asked 'em. They thought I was joking; I guess this place was built last century. Since I like to lay a bet or two on the horses, I asked the old woman to bring me in a mobile. We're not supposed to use 'em in case they upsets equipment, but I don't reckon I've stopped anything. If you'd like to use mine, you're welcome."

"You'd be doing me a good turn."

"I reckon it's best not to let 'em see what one's doing, so I get me head under the bedclothes. If they hears me talking, they just think I'm losing me marbles."

He was passed a mobile telephone after the other had inserted the PIN number. He went to duck under the bedclothes forgetting that sudden action was inadvisable and gasped as fresh liquid fire raced up and down his side. When that had died down to mere agony, he very carefully hunched his head under the sheet and single blanket and began to dial, discovered he'd become so fumble-fisted it took him three attempts before he correctly completed the task. He pressed OK. The phone rang. One of the female civilian operators at divisional HQ answered the call and he asked to be put through to Cain.

"It's Mike, Sarge."

"How's things?" Cain asked, clearly not wanting to be told and hoping the call would be brief and of no consequence.

"I'm in hospital because some bastard tried to run me down, but only succeeded in slamming me up against another car."

"Are you on the booze?"

"Should I be so lucky? I think it was a Mercedes saloon – one of the big ones – and it was black. Two of the registration numbers were either OF or OE. I couldn't manage better than that."

"You're not having me on?"

"I'm in Crick General . . . Hang on." He slowly eased his head out into the open. "What ward is this?"

"Five A, mate."

He returned under the bedclothes. "Ward Five A."

"I'll get someone along."

"There's nothing more I can tell."

"Maybe you'll remember something when you try."

How often had he said that to a victim and believed it to be true? He switched off the mobile, handed it back with his thanks, lay back, closed his eyes, and tried to picture the car as he had seen it, driving away. But images refused to form. He drifted off into a sleep which seemed to last only seconds before he was jerked awake by his thoughts. He raised his wrist to look at his watch, found it was not there. Smashed in the collision? He spoke to the man on his right. "What's the time?"

"Just after four, mate. Give it a bit longer and I'll know if I've had any luck at Newmarket."

"Can I borrow your mobile again?"

"Help yourself."

"I'll settle with you for the calls."

"No sweat. I don't pay for 'em."

As he took the mobile, he wondered if the other would have been quite so forthright if he'd known to whom he was speaking. Certainly not if the phone was cloned and the cost of the calls was appearing on someone else's account. He hoped for the sake of justice that that was not the explanation. He slipped under the bedclothes once more and dialled.

"Six one five four," Fay said.

"It's Mike and—"

"You bastard! You double-tailed bastard!"

"Hang on—"

"Hang you, more like. You listen to me. Until now, I've been on your side because I couldn't believe you were the prize sod you've now proved yourself to be. I kept telling Anne, all husbands are near impossible. Maybe you did come home late and had forgotten to read to Judy, but if that was the worst you ever got up to, she could count herself lucky. I reminded her how she'd caught you secretly comforting Judy when she'd been sent to her bedroom for being naughty and it brought a lump to her throat. I got her so misty-eyed she wondered if you were eating enough. When she discovered you were coming to lunch today – Judy couldn't keep the secret, despite the chocolates – she didn't start shouting she'd clear off to London, she became even more misty-eyed and her conscience began to dig deeper. Then what happens? Ifor opens the first bottle and we sip. And we sip. And the bubbles start to peter out. And by one thirty, Anne's up in her bedroom, weeping; and if she'd any sense, swearing that if she ever speaks to you again, it'll only be to tell you precisely who and what you are. As for me – I hope you end up with a bottle blonde who can't cook and watches soaps except when she's entertaining the milkman."

"You wouldn't like to hear why I didn't turn up for lunch?"

"No. I have a delicate mind."

"I was . . ." To say an attempt had been made to murder him must cause panic. "I had an accident."

"You stubbed your big toe in the hurry to avoid the returning husband?"

"I was about to drive over to you when a car hit me. You'll be sorry to hear that the only damage seems to be heavy bruising."

There was a silence. Then: "Is this a typical male lie to try to excuse your appalling behaviour?"

"Come and see me in hospital if you won't believe me."

"You're in hospital?"

"As I would have told you at the beginning if you hadn't gone for me all ends up."

"Won't have done you any harm. Like Ifor, you've never understood what a treasure you're married to . . . What hospital are you in?"

"Crick General. Ward Five A."

"Damn, I can't find a pencil. Why is nothing ever where it should be? What ward?"

"Five A."

"I'll tell Ifor to go in one of the cars and find Anne. She's out on a walk with Judy . . . What do you want her to bring you?"

"Nothing. The doc says I should be out tomorrow."

"When she's with you, moan from time to time. It'll arouse her maternal instincts."

"What if those aren't the ones I want to arouse?"

"Then you're not nearly as injured as you're trying to make out."

Parr breezed into the ward and eyed the more attractive nurse in sight as he walked over to Keen's bed. "You look like you've had a heavy night," was his comforting greeting. He sat on the chair between the beds. "The sarge sends his best wishes."

"In the circumstances, that's generous of him."

"I don't suppose he meant it. So how are things?"

"I'm surviving."

"What's the damage?"

"Heavy bruising."

"Is that all?"

"You don't think it's enough?"

"When I got smashed up in the game against A Division last season, I broke a collarbone and a rib."

"I'm sorry to be so unimpressive."

"Is that right what you told the sarge, the car tried to run you down?"

"Actually, I said it was the driver."

"How d'you mean?"

"Never mind."

Parr looked at a nurse who'd just entered the ward. "You've some reasonable talent here. She could bandage my strained groin any time . . . Why are you so sure the car was after you?"

Keen described what had happened

"Couldn't it have been a joyrider who thought he was Schumacher but found he wasn't?"

"When the car drove off, it wasn't weaving across the road and it was accelerating. If a joyrider loses it and smashes into someone, he'll instinctively be braking and even more out of control."

"Maybe someone with too many pints under his belly?"

"The same applies."

"I suppose you could be right . . . But you failed to get the number?"

"Two of the letters were OF or OE."

"That's not going to take us very far."

"Next time, I'll forget I might be bleeding to death and concentrate on the number."

Parr's attention again wandered as the nurse walked past.

Anne crossed the ward to the bed, hesitated, leaned over and kissed him on the cheek. She straightened up. "Fay says you've been badly bruised, but nothing's broken?"

"That's the picture."

"Is the bruising very painful?"

"Bearable when I remember not to move too quickly."

"Judy says to give you her love and get well very soon."

"Tell her thanks and I will."

She sat. "I didn't bring you anything because you told Fay there was nothing you wanted."

"There didn't seem much point since with any luck I'll be home tomorrow . . . I just couldn't make lunch."

"For heaven's sake, of course you couldn't."

"I phoned as soon as I could pull my wits together."

"Mike, I understand."

"But you sound . . . Fay seemed to suggest . . ." How could he tell her when the men on either side of him could listen to what he said if they chose to do so?

"I've tried to make her understand how things really are, but she won't listen. She sees things as she wants them to be." She spoke with a restraint that matched his. "It's awful seeing you lying there." She stared at the wall above his head as she said: "But that doesn't change things."

There was a long silence, then their conversation became carefully neutral. When she left, he wondered if Fay would ever realise what bitterness her romantic optimism could engender?

Twenty-Two

B y Friday, Keen had recovered sufficiently to drive to
divisional HQ. When he entered the DI's room. Drew's
expression tightened, but his greeting was cordial. "Good to
see you back on your feet."

"Thank you, sir."

"But don't stay on them any longer than you have to. Grab
a seat."

Keen set a chair in front of the desk. "I've been wondering if
there's any joy in tracing the car which ran me down?"

Drew picked up a sheet of paper. "We contacted all forces
and asked for details of cars stolen on the Tuesday, Wednesday, or early Thursday morning. On the Wednesday, a black
Mercedes two eighty was stolen from the drive of a house in
Kingsley Heath, which is approximately twenty miles from
Birmingham. Having been registered locally, two of its four
letters were one of the alternatives you quoted. It was discovered in a deserted quarry, having been torched."

"A repeat of the Noyes case! That has to be the car that tried
to kill me. Searle had a contract on me because I was getting
too close to exposing him."

"Where's the proof that the driver of the car was trying to
run you down rather than that he negligently lost control?"

"Because he drove off in full control after he'd hit me."

"At that moment, neither your judgement nor your vision
could have been at its sharpest."

"What if they weren't? Since it can't be a coincidence that in

203

both cases the same MO was used, there's no room for argument."

"A sharp lawyer always finds room. Where's the proof that this incident, whatever its nature, was in any way connected with Noyes's death; that Searle had any part in it or knows about it even now?"

"Forget legal proof and the need to dot every i and cross every t. Common sense says that's the way it was."

"The Crown Prosecution Service has little time for common sense. It also dislikes cases where there's less than a fifty-fifty chance of a successful prosecution."

"And you wouldn't be boosting your career if they turned the case down."

"You've been under severe strain so I'll forget you said that."

"Be my guest and remember it as much as you like. I've a very personal interest in this. They've tried to kill me and failed, so it's a hundred to one that they'll try again and this time make certain they succeed."

"There's no reason to think that."

"From where I am, there's every reason. Searle knows it's because I pushed so hard that he's in the frame; obviously he reckons that if I'm removed, he'll be allowed to drop out of sight. People will become more concerned about their own careers."

Drew began to rub his chin. "You seem to suffer the delusion that you're the only person who is capable and willing to pursue justice."

"I've learned that justice means different things to different persons."

"It means only one thing in this force."

"In theory, not in practice . . . Has there been any progress in the Chambers murder?"

"None that I know of," Drew replied tightly.

"Then if I'm to stand any chance of enjoying my next birthday, Searle's bank accounts must be checked."

"In the present circumstances, that is an impossibility."

"The present circumstances are, he's tried to have me murdered."

"Yet again, there is not one shred of proof to support that accusation."

"There would be if anyone here had the courage to follow up the facts."

"Rules have to be observed."

"Especially when it's a case of self-preservation . . . Where do I stand now?"

"Where you stood before."

"I'm still suspended?"

"The facts leading to your suspension haven't altered."

"Or your willingness to face the truth." Keen stood. "I have the feeling that if they manage to get me, your conscience won't be disturbed for too long."

There was no parking space in Craythorne Road, but there was in the next road. Keen locked the Astra and then walked up the passage which brought him to the narrow dirt lane which ran between the two rows of houses. He opened the gate into his back garden, went up the gravel path to the back door, took the key out of his pocket, found the door was unlocked. So concerned about the forthcoming meeting with Drew, he must have forgotten to lock it. Yet thinking back, he remembered leaving by the front door because his car was parked in Craythorne Road . . . Believing he'd enter by the front door, had the back one been left unlocked to provide an emergency way of escape by someone inside who was waiting to stick a knife into his guts or tighten a noose around his neck?

He opened the door slowly. He stepped into the kitchen, stood still and listened intently. Silence. He took off his shoes and in stockinged feet crossed to the inside door, which was open, and looked into the hall. Empty. He stepped into the hall and as he did so heard a brief sound of movement from the sitting room. He now knew where the would-be murderer was waiting.

Foot by foot, then inch by inch, he approached the door. He gripped the handle and slowly turned it until the lock was under full tension. He took a deep breath and then, shouting at the top of his voice, flung open the door and rushed in, arms held ready for immediate violent action.

Anne, seated in an armchair, screamed. "My God, Mike!"

He came to a stop. "What the hell are you doing here?" he demanded violently.

"Mike, you've near made me wet my knickers from fright!"

"What are you doing here?"

She regained a measure of calm. "It's nice to discover how much I'm appreciated. I suppose there's someone upstairs who doesn't know I exist and you're trying to warn her."

"There's no one upstairs."

His answer surprised her.

"Why did you come here?" he asked yet again.

She said slowly: "To find out the truth."

"About what?"

"I was in town and ran into Len. He told me not to worry, they were doing everything possible to identify whoever it was had tried to kill you. When he realised I'd no idea what he was talking about, he began spluttering that he'd made a mistake. But he hadn't. You weren't hurt in an ordinary accident, were you?"

"Of course I was. As usual, Len's got everything completely muddled. The driver of the car was talking on a mobile and lost his concentration . . ."

"After scaring me half to death, you seemed furious to find me in the house, so naturally I thought you'd someone . . . But you were angry because you were scared. That's the truth, isn't it?"

He crossed to a chair and slumped down on it.

206

"Please, you've got to tell me. Why were you so frightened to find me here?"

Not to answer would cause her more distress, because her imagination would have no boundaries, than if she knew the facts. "You may now be in danger."

"Why? How?"

He briefly told her the facts.

"Oh, my God! . . . Why won't Mr Drew believe you?"

"To do so doesn't suit his career prospects . . . That's not being wholly fair. He's right in one respect. There isn't any solid proof, only endless circumstantial evidence which can't yet be tied in."

"But if he made certain the bank accounts were examined, there would be that proof?"

"There might be. It's a gamble which he wasn't prepared to take in his own name before and certainly won't now, when to do so would make it seem very likely that he had encouraged me."

"He's putting his career above your life?"

"He wouldn't see things in that light."

"Because he doesn't want to!"

"Don't we all see only what we want to? I thought of us all as a team – one for all, all for one. But both he and the sarge have made it all too obvious that team loyalty only lasts until the going gets tough; then it's a case of each man for himself. If I'd listened to common sense, I'd never have imagined it to be otherwise."

"Be proud, not scornful, that you were fooled."

"Proud of putting you and Judy at risk?"

"How can we be?"

"Because . . . We both need a drink."

"You've got to tell me."

"With a gin in my hand. What do you want?"

For a moment it looked as if she wouldn't answer, then she said: "Whisky."

207

He went through to the larder and poured out a whisky and soda and a gin and tonic. Back in the sitting room, he handed her one glass, sat.

"Well?" she demanded.

"Since they decided to kill me by running me down and making it seem an accident, they must have been keeping the house under surveillance to determine whether I had a discernible routine and which was my car. When they were ready, they had a try at killing me, but I was lucky. Their next action will likely be straightforward, with no attempt to try to make it look a possible accident. It could be firebombs through the windows in the middle of the night or an explosive that brings the whole house down; but I reckon they'll be slightly more subtle than that. All the time they've been watching this place I've been on my own, so unless they've asked questions locally – which is unlikely as they'll have wanted to stay deep in the shadows – they won't have known I'm married and have a daughter. But you coming here has suggested I have a wife or girlfriend, so they'll have tried to check who you are by breaking into your car and reading though any papers they find. Is there anything in your car that will identify who you are and where you're staying?"

"There are the usual car papers."

"Which will tell them you're my wife, but thankfully give this address. Nothing else?"

"No . . . Yes."

"What?"

"I think I left a letter from Hazel on the passenger seat and it's addressed care of Fay."

"Then we must assume they do now know where you're living," he said harshly. "And I don't doubt that in the letter Hazel asks how Judy is?" He looked at Anne.

She nodded.

"So they also know I have a daughter. Which means they have the bait to set the trap for a subtle murder."

"You've got to make Mr Drew stop them," she said, her voice shrill.

"He can do nothing until they're identified. At the moment only Searle can do that. Which he very obviously is not going to do."

"So are you just going to sit there and go on and on saying what can't be done?"

"No."

She gripped her hands together. "I'm sorry, Mike. Of course you'll do something . . . But what? In God's name, what?"

Twenty-Three

The London offices of the Aylton Shipping Company were in an area of London once traditionally devoted to the sea; they failed to follow further tradition since there was not one meticulously detailed model of a ship anywhere.

Keen walked up to the counter in the large reception area on the ground floor. One of the three women working at computers stood and crossed to where he waited. "How can I help you?"

"I'd like to speak to Mr Searle."

"Have you an appointment?"

"No, I don't."

"Then I rather doubt he'll be able to see you. But I can have a word with his secretary?"

"If you would. The name's Keen."

She returned to her workstation, picked up a phone, pressed one of the dialling buttons and spoke briefly. Returning to the counter, she said: "I'm afraid she says he's very busy and can't see you."

There was a door at the far end of the area and, to the accompaniment of ever more agitated calls, he crossed to it, opened it, and went through. Beyond was a narrow passage, lit by a low-wattage bulb, and a flight of stairs. He climbed these to reach a corridor on either side of which were three frosted-glass doors. One of them opened and a middle-aged man, wearing half-moon glasses, stepped out. "What are you doing?" he asked, in a voice which carried more concern than authority.

"I'm looking for Mr Searle's office."

He instinctively looked to his right, then back. As Keen walked past him, he said petulantly: "You can't go in there . . ."

Above the end right-hand door was, in brass, the legend, "Chairman". Keen opened the door and entered. Chairmen often favoured offices spacious enough to overawe. Searle did not. But anyone who knew something about furniture would have been impressed by the Victorian mahogany pedestal desk and the Georgian breakfront bookcase with broken pediment.

Searle was seated at the desk and standing by his side was a middle-aged woman holding a folder in her hands. They stared at him, Searle's expression enigmatic, the woman's surprised.

"I said to tell him you were busy," she said.

"That's all right, Miss Chalmers. If you'll do the letter right away," Searle said. "And don't forget to ring Cairo and find out what the present situation is."

"Don't you want . . ." she began uncertainly.

"Thank you, no."

She crossed to the door, looked briefly at Keen, her expression one of perplexity, left.

"Why have you've walked in here after being told I was too busy to see you?" Searle asked, his tone even.

"To persuade you to call off the contract to kill me."

"That proposition is as ridiculous as your previous assertion that I killed a steward on the *Slecome Bay* and recently ordered the murder of . . . What was the man's name?"

"Noyes."

"Of course."

"Presumably, what you really find ridiculous is that I should be able to walk into here. Having chosen a top team, you expected me to be long since dead."

Searle opened a chased silver cigarette box that was the twin of the one in Mierton Manor. "Do you smoke?"

"No."

"Of course you don't. You told me so on a previous occasion. Old men forget."

"Most especially those things they prefer not to remember."

"Perhaps. Now, you were going to explain the reason for this unannounced visit."

"I already have."

"And if I tell you that I haven't the slightest idea what you're talking about?"

"I'll call you a liar."

"That is your privilege, but like most privileges, it can cause resentment . . . Constable, I have not asked anyone to kill you. I have no reason to do so and even if I had, I would not countenance doing such a thing. And perhaps it is pertinent to add that I've no idea how to go about making so unusual a request."

"And the moon's made of blue cheese. Continue to feign ignorance and we'll both end up in the shit; agree I'm to stay alive and you'll continue to fool almost all the people almost all of the time."

"To my regret, since I dislike causing trouble, I've previously had to make an informal complaint about your behaviour; leave now and I'll forget this incident, otherwise I'll have to lay a formal complaint which will, I imagine, bring an end to your career."

"You won't voluntarily agree to call off the contract?"

"Have I not made myself clear?"

Keen paused for a moment. Everything – his life, his future and that of his family – counted on the next few minutes' conversation.

"Your wife is a major shareholder in the company, isn't she?"

Searle's eyes narrowed. "And if she is?"

"Then your position as chairman rests on her supporting you. So if she had reason to cause you as much harm as possible, she'd be able to force you out of office?"

Searle finally took a cigarette out of the box and lit it.

"It's obvious she values social standing very highly. I've read that you're in line for a life peerage. Lady Searle. How the name will trip off her tongue! But there's one problem to scaling the heights – the only way forward is down. So if you're exposed as a murderer who killed in sordid circumstances, she'll remain plain Mrs Searle, her minor royal friends will royally snub her, and even the butcher, baker, and candlestick maker will have the temerity to treat her as an equal."

"Does it satisfy a sense of inferiority to insult my wife?"

"If I'd wanted to insult her, I'd have been very much more specific. What I've just said is simple fact. There's nothing the social set enjoys more than seeing one of their number in trouble."

"Even if correct, that is hardly relevant."

"Very relevant when the evidence of your bank statements shows you were paying blackmail to Noyes."

"My solicitors assure me that there is not a shred of evidence sufficient to warrant a display order being granted."

"There's evidence all right."

"There is none because none exists."

"It exists, but the criminal law demands more than can at present be produced."

"The same thing."

"Not exactly."

Searle stubbed out his cigarette. "I have repeatedly tried to convince you of the stupidity of your accusations, but you've equally repeatedly refused to listen. You leave me with no alternative other than to instruct my solicitors to take all necessary steps to prevent this ridiculous harassment continuing."

"Before you do that, consider one important fact."

"What?"

"The standard of evidence required in a civil case is different from that in a criminal one."

"I fail to see that that is of the slightest consequence."

"The first attempt on my life failed, but unless the contract is called off there will be a second and probably successful one. My wife and daughter could well be victims. To prevent that possibility, I'll do whatever I have to. So I've drawn up a résumé of all the facts, coincidences, possibilities, and probabilities, and explained how they link together. Anyone who reads this can have no doubt that you murdered Orr, ordered Noyes's murder, and tried to have me murdered."

"I'll obtain an injunction preventing your publishing such insulting nonsense."

"I won't be publishing in the old-fashioned sense. I'll put it on the Internet and there's no way you or anyone else can stop me doing that. Inevitably, the media will pick it up and give the details maximum publicity. When these become common knowledge, you'll have to decide whether to ignore the fuss or sue me for libel. Ignore it and the great British public, delighted to denigrate anyone who has achieved success, will name you a murderer. Take me to court on a civil action for libel and much of the evidence a criminal court would hold inadmissible will be accepted and some of the evidence not yet to hand will have to be disclosed by court order. So either way, you'll be damned. And Mrs Searle, plain Mrs Searle, will have a husband who was indulging in a homosexual affair when engaged to her. I don't think one need wonder how a woman of her nature will react to the amused notoriety this will engender."

"Presumably, you now intend to try to blackmail me?"

"Not in the conventional sense."

"You will term every payment from me a gift in order to salve your conscience?"

"I want the contract on me called off and for you to inform the Chief Constable that you withdraw your complaint regarding the attempt to examine your bank accounts because you've remembered that you gave me permission for that."

"You think I'd be believed?"

"No. But because it will make life easier for everyone, your lie will be gratefully accepted."

"What are your other demands?"

"There are none."

"Blackmailers are never content."

"You have the full price of my silence."

"If I agree to pay, I'll have placed myself in a position of guilt. Sooner or later, you'll tell me you'd like a few tens of thousands to make life more comfortable."

"You have my word I will demand nothing further."

"Very poor security."

"Then rely on your tapes."

"What tapes?"

"You'll have been recording this conversation so you have me admitting to a kind of blackmail and if you made that admission public, I would be thrown out of the force and charged. So it is in my interest not to provoke you as it is in your interest not to provoke me. What better guarantee could there be that each of us will keep his word as a gentleman?"

Searle said slowly: "If ever you decide to leave the police and enter business, I imagine you will be highly successful."

Twenty-Four

A s Keen opened the front door, Anne, her face lined by worry, hurried into the hall. "What happened?"

"It's all right. He'll call off the contract."

"Oh, my God! Oh, my God!"

About to go forward to comfort her, he checked himself, uncertain how she would react to physical contact.

"Judy's safe?"

"You both are."

"And you?"

"Me too."

"I knew you'd succeed."

"Then, frankly, you knew more than I did. He might have decided he'd be able to hire lawyers clever or twisted enough to make certain he ended up in the clear. Money can wipe clear most any dirt."

"What happens to him?"

"Nothing."

"But he's responsible for the deaths of two people."

"The possibility of proving he murdered Orr was always very slim. Noyes was a blackmailer."

"Does that make any difference?"

"The law holds every life is equally valuable, life proves it isn't. In any case, he already has a life sentence to serve. He has Berenice as his wife."

She produced a small lace-edged handkerchief and wiped

her eyes. "I'm living up to male tradition and crying because I'm so happy . . . Come on."

"Where to?"

She didn't answer, but left. He followed her into the kitchen. "It's in the refrigerator," she said. "On the bottom shelf."

He brought out a bottle of Mumm. "You could be that certain I'd succeed?"

"You'd promised me you would."

Faith unfaithfully kept.

They were in the sitting room, drinking their first glass of champagne, when she said, speaking a shade too casually, "There was a phone call for you, but the caller wouldn't give me her name."

He wondered why life ensured that the unwanted happened at the worst possible moment?

"However, I imagine you'll know who she was."

"Probably Laura Ellis. She's Noyes's niece."

"She seemed surprised when I said I was your wife."

He could imagine.

"You've not been too lonely, then?"

"You're wondering if I've been sleeping with her?"

"Of course not."

"I haven't.' There could be a time when the truth was whatever the listener most wanted to hear. "Nor did I ever make a play. Our pheromones don't dance together. And I wouldn't have been able to compete with the ghost."

"Ghost?"

"Of her recently deceased husband. Finally, she has an impossible daughter who would debud any budding romance."

She twisted the stem of her champagne flute between forefinger and thumb. "The wrong scent, a ghost, and an obnoxious daughter. The poor woman."

"But richer in worldly goods through meeting me. Because now that there'll never be proof any part of what Noyes owned at his death came from blackmail, all his estate will be hers."

"So if she finds a different scent, lays the ghost to rest, and puts her daughter in boarding school, you could find her attractive?"

"When one's drunk champagne, cider is a poor substitute."

"Cap the bottle, Mike, and we'll finish it when we get back."

"Back from where?"

"Fetching Judy."

"Are . . . Are you returning home?"

"We've both learned something which must change our lives together. Drew and the sergeant kicked you into the mud because they feared that if they didn't they'd land in it themselves. So you've had to understand that for most people, team loyalty lasts only as long as it doesn't threaten. I've had to understand I was so bloody wrong to accuse you of never thinking of anyone but yourself. When you blackmailed Searle, you were betraying everything you hold worthwhile for mine and Judy's sake. And I don't care what you said a moment ago, you hated doing it."

He stood and crossed the carpet. He brought out of his pocket the small, gift-wrapped box. "For you."

She undid the paper, lifted the lid, stared at the silver brooch. "Tyke! It's Tyke! Oh, my God, Mike, kiss me before I start crying so hard you'll have a shower if you come too close."